THE BATHSHEBA CONNECTION

Ruth Walter

Writers Club Press

San Jose New York Lincoln Shanghai

The Bathsheba Connection

Published by Writers Club Press
an imprint of iUniverse.com, Inc.

For information address:
iUniverse.com, Inc.
620 North 48th Street
Suite 201
Lincoln, NE 68504-3467
www.iuniverse.com

ISBN: 0-595-09325-6

Printed in the United States of America

CHAPTER ONE

I was living in Paris, the city of my dreams, when suddenly one night I got tangled up in a murder. To put it more accurately, I tangled myself up in a murder.

On that momentous night, I, Goldie Yampolsky, retired special ed teacher and failed painter from New York, was trying to sleep in our IKEA bed on the top floor of our two level apartment in the Marais section of Paris. Our balcony bedroom was as hot and humid as the belly button of hell—the Marais used to be a swamp in the olden days. It still is, come to think of it, a swamp of lost humanity. Excuse the generalization.

Anyway, I was awakened by a heart-rending shriek from I didn't know where. In New York I wouldn't have paid attention. But this was Paris and I was already acquainted with some of the neighbors, and it sounded like one of them needed my help. Should I deny them? I ran down our inside stairs to the living room and looked out the window to the cobbled street. Nothing. The only light came from the workroom of the all-night dress designer across the way who was hunched over his drawing board, oblivious.

I ran into the den behind the living room. The cries were definitely coming from one of the apartments on the courtyard, but which? I ran back up the stairs to where Sol was sleeping like a baby in spite of the screams. He was on his back, his curly brown and gray hair damp on the pillow—snoring. He's such a sound sleeper he doesn't wake up even when I give a push to turn him over.

I craned my neck over the rooftops and chimney pots until I saw, across the courtyard, to my horror, the top half of Veronique being shoved out the window. Big, hairy hands were strangling her. She was screaming and struggling.

Just that afternoon I had tea with her when Sol was in the library at the Pompidou Center. We discussed famous writers and artists she had known when she was a model. Besides being smart, she was gorgeous, with brown eyes and that short, shiny black hair we used to call a Patsy-doll cut when I was a kid. And such a nice person. Who was doing this to her? Whose hands were those? I didn't ponder over it.

"You stop that!" I'm yelling in English—my French is inadequate to the situation. The rest of the courtyard is still playing rock music or sleeping, or maybe eating, and is singularly disinterested. In this I am reminded of New York.

"Leave her alone or I'll call the cops, les police!" How could I do that with my limited French? The screaming stopped and the window slammed down. But who knows what's going on behind it?

"Sol, wake up. Somebody is murdering Veronique!"

Sol is lying there a bump on a log. What can I do? I shake him. He doesn't budge. I'm wasting time. I have to do something to help her. No one else will. I am out the door, running down the circular staircase of rough red stones. Well not exactly running, but going as fast as I can down five flights. I'm not so young as I was and I don't want to stumble and land on my head. Madame Goldie Yampolsky wouldn't be much help to anybody then, would I? I'm scurrying like a mouse in a maze without even a bathrobe over my nightie.

At the bottom, I see a blur of cloth, I don't know what, in the arcade outside the iron gate, near the Russian art gallery. But the blur is too fast-moving and I'm not sure if it's a person or trash blowing in the wind. I don't have time to investigate. I am rushing through the courtyard and up the stairs of the back building, batiment B, to the sixth floor-one apartment to a floor like in batiment A, where I live. I stop in front of an open door, panting, my heart jumping out of my chest. Thank God I don't have to open the door and leave my fingerprints on it. I don't know what made me think of such a thing at a moment like that.

No more screaming. Only ominous stillness heavy in the air. I tiptoe into the living room.

Lying on the floor is a dead person.

A male dead person.

A surprise.

I give myself a moment of relief that it's not Veronique. Then I make myself look at what was once a living face. I recognize the profile. Veronique's husband Jacques Ombre. I know he's dead from the staring look in his eye and the amount of blood turning his blond hair red and making rivers on his black leather jacket. One sleeve is hiked up so I see part of a blue crucifix tattooed on his arm. The rest of the artwork is hidden. Though I'm not too accustomed to viewing dead people, I have seen enough make-believe ones in the movies to know dead. I also know I shouldn't touch anything.

Who is this husband of Veronique, this Jacques Ombre, when he's not strangling women? An enigma. Veronique never talked about him. Sol thinks he's a pimp or a drug dealer. I wouldn't go so far. But he does look to me like some kind of petty crook, though I wouldn't accuse without evidence. But whoever he was, he isn't anymore. He's dead now and no great loss to Veronique from what I saw happening in her window.

In the house of my mind there is a camera. If I tell my mind to do it, it will take a picture of anything I want. Later, when I wish, I can retrieve the images. I give the order. The camera focuses on the tall mahogany grandfather clock inlaid with gold angels. Then it pans to the sofa with its curlicued wood frame, its gold brocade covering, and cushions slumbering peacefully at the corners. Ivory colored drapes hang over the open back window, shaking in the breeze.

Framed Man Ray photos, a small Picasso. Antiques. I click my camera on all of them. I don't know periods. I only know quality. And the quality of the furniture and art is superior to the quality of the apartment, believe me.

Except for the trashy bronze statue of a woman washing her feet. A piece of junk like they sell in the flea market. Who am I to judge? The important thing is that the statue is splashed with blood. The murder weapon? I'm sure of it. But bronze is heavy—even in a not-so-big statue like this. Veronique could never pick it up to hit someone, especially if she's being strangled. I have the desire to try to lift it and see—but the common sense not to. Common sense also tells me to get the heck out of there or something terrible might happen to me.

But I stay. I allow myself another minute of relief that Veronique is not the victim—or the murderer. She's a doll and wouldn't do such a thing even if she could.

I hear something like a sigh, I don't know what. I have a sinking feeling. I'm suddenly afraid she's somewhere in the apartment hurt, or God forbid, also dead. I'm starting to tremble. But I'm an addicted snoop. I can't help myself. I take a look in the bedroom, the bathroom, the kitchen. Thank God she's not in any of those rooms. I hear something like a whisper behind the drapes. I push them aside with my elbow and look out over the Picasso—like rooftops. I see only a piece of moon flickering high up in the sky. It tells me nothing. I turn to look through the window that faces our apartment, but the shade is pulled down.

As for me, I was where I shouldn't be. Who knows, maybe the murderer was beyond my vision on a rooftop, watching—waiting to pounce? It was time to go. I stumbled over an empty wine bottle. I thought the label might be important and was about to kick it over when I heard what sounded like a cough. It could have been anything. I didn't wait around to see.

I also didn't want to risk being seen—not that I was guilty of anything-except nosiness. I ran as quietly as I could down the wooden stairs. I knew that I should go immediately to the police station and tell them what I heard and saw. But where was the police station? And how could I communicate?

I didn't know I could move so fast. I ran through the courtyard, and only slowed down when I was going up the ancient circular stairs to our apartment. I wondered what time it was. I wondered why I was wondering. It couldn't be after two a.m. because the dogs in the apartment below us were still barking. They always bark until their masters come home from the restaurant where they work. This doesn't bother Sol as he can sleep through any kind of noise—the house could be on fire and the sirens wouldn't wake him.

But he was almost awake and sitting up when I got into the bed next to him. It was my absence that was waking him. My solid presence beside him is necessary to keep him in the arms of Morpheus.

"Where were you, Goldie? I thought you were kidnapped." This was Sol's recurrent nightmare when we lived on the Upper West Side and I insisted on going out alone at night to French classes—a lot of good they did me.

"You won't believe this…" I told him what happened, but I didn't know if he heard—he kept falling asleep, then jerking himself awake. But he heard the sirens—because I kicked him hard when those howls swirled up and in through the front windows, followed by urgent voices and the sound of feet on the cobblestones of the street and courtyard.

"What did you do now, Goldie?"

"Why do you always assume when there is trouble that I am responsible? What could I do?"

"You could stick your nose where it doesn't belong. You usually do."

"Veronique was being strangled out the window. What else could I do? I ran to help her."

"And did you?"

"I was too late."

"So there you are. What do you mean too late?"

"There was a dead body in the apartment."

"Veronique?"

"No. Her husband. But she didn't do it."

"How do you know?"

"Because she's petite. She couldn't lift that bronze statue. She could maybe lift it a little, but not enough to hit him in the head, and anyway not when he was strangling her."

"Goldie, you saw all that?" There was a look of pity in his soft gray eyes. More for me than Veronique, or her husband who he had taken a dislike to on sight.

"Did anyone see you go in there?"

"I don't think so. Actually no one could have. There's no other apartment on the floor. Maybe someone saw me in the courtyard or running up the stairs, but I doubt it. Everybody is too busy with their own thing to worry about someone else, and anyway that doesn't prove anything. God, I sound guilty."

"You can't help it. It's in the genes."

"Solly, I was the only one who tried to stop it."

"I know. It's very difficult for you not to help someone when they are in trouble, even when they don't ask for help, even when your help gets them in worse trouble. I understand your caring motivation, Lady of the Lamp, but this is not your country. If the natives don't care why should you?"

"The Crimea wasn't Florence Nightingale's either."

"Why do I try? I can't change your nature, and I wouldn't want to. Hey Goldilocks. Take care of yourself. I love you."

I always get embarrassed when Sol talks like that. Even when we are alone. I still don't believe that handsome high school athlete fell for me, a nobody, who was always by myself, sketching, while the popular girls were flirting and running after him. A baseball scout wanted to sign him up for a minor league team, but in those days it paid peanuts, and besides Jews were supposed to be doctors or lawyers, not ball players, never mind Hank Greenberg.

"Goldilocks, I think it's time to go home."

"I am home," I told him. And I was.

My desire to live in Paris had been an ache in my side ever since I was an art student preparing to become the greatest painter of the century-well anyway, a painter. It didn't happen. But Paris finally did, long after the petals of my youth dropped off and smothered my hopes for a romantic Bohemian life.

"I mean home to America. We only need to give three months notice. I would even forfeit the rent."

As you can see, Sol wasn't so happy in the role of expatriate. To be honest, he hated it. He didn't talk much about it, that's not his way, but even then a rash was sprouting on his chest and creeping upward. I believed, and still do, that if we stay in Paris long enough, Sol will include in his amorous thoughts, not only his American mistresses, the New York Yankees, and the old St. Louis Cardinals, but Paris herself—the Seine, the parks, the museums, the old buildings, and so forth. At that moment, he was drawn only to the gorgeous, but smelly French coquette, Notre Dame de Paris. But he would abandon her in a shot if I agreed to go back to New York.

Poor Sol, I know he's homesick. He misses his kids, his grandchildren, the New York Public Library, and baseball. There's no baseball on French TV, which we don't have anyway, and inadequate coverage in the International Herald Tribune. He feels cheated he can't spend his retirement in the Yankee stadium though he didn't go there for years because of crime in the area. I know I'm depriving him, but he had his way for forty years and now it's my turn.

Let me tell you about me from my point of view—which is not necessarily someone else's. I raised three kids and, like a good New York mother, messed up their lives, or so they said. Now that they were perfectly capable of doing it themselves, I flew the coop. I said goodbye to the Upper West Side of Manhattan—to the violence that surrounded but ignored me. In Paris there wasn't so much violence but what there was welcomed me where I lived on the two top floors of a tenement in the lower depths of rue Abbe Etienne.

"You didn't give Paris a chance, Solly. A little more time and you might adjust, even enjoy living here. We could always move to a quieter apartment."

"I'll consider it. Get some sleep."

"I'll try."

But I couldn't. I kept seeing Jacques Ombre's face haloed by blood. I kept wondering where Veronique was and worrying about her. My thoughts were doing battle with sleep. In the courtyard I could hear the policemen, and from the apartment below, a symphony of barking dogs.

A miracle, Sol also couldn't sleep.

"How about a cup of tea?" I asked him.

"Why not?"

We had tea. It was my last leisurely cup of tea in donkey's years, as the Brits say on BBC radio.

CHAPTER TWO

The next morning, almost cross-eyed from fatigue, I negotiated the rough stone stairs of batiment A on my way to rue Rambuteau for fresh croissants au beurre. In the courtyard I passed important looking people heading for the stairs of Batiment B, carrying important looking cases. The police cars and pompiers and ambulances that had clogged the narrow street the night before were gone, except for the one patrol car on the corner with its two rumpled occupants sipping coffee out of plastic cups and harassing newspapers.

The patrol car wasn't causing problems since this section of rue Abbe Etienne is a semi-walking street with only the occasional car. The major traffic on the block is the large wagon loaded with folded boxes for the warehouse across the street, schlepped every few days by our resident clochard—or homeless drunk—who was ragged and dirty. Even his blond, Rastafarian hairdo was turning earth color, and stuck out in all directions around a face like a child's playdough ashtray.

Rue Abbe Etienne is a street in transition. If you're standing where it intersects rue Rambuteau and looking in the direction of the Pompidou Center, you see expensive restaurants, elegant boutiques, and famous art galleries. If you look the other way toward our building, you see a narrowing street with centuries old crumbling facades in cubistic shapes and shades of gray and tan. The street looks like the movie set for "The Cabinet of Dr. Caligari," and, as I was to learn later, some of the people who lived there might well have escaped from Caligari's lunatic asylum. As for the others, they were a mixture of poor folks, mostly North Africans, and Yuppies in newly gentrified apartments.

Our part of the street had a working class cafe and our building had a gallery on the ground floor specializing in Russian art. It was hardly ever open, and I wouldn't have known the owner if I passed him in the street. Actually, I don't believe I ever saw him.

Around the time Jacques Ombre was murdered, I was already acquainted with a few of the neighborhood characters. Some I knew by sight, some from gossip, and others from the conversations we had. For example, the hurdy-gurdy woman, who brought her instrument out each morning and polished it before setting out for her street concerts, always gave weather forecasts, and she was always right.

She was a tall Breton woman, with a craggy masculine face, like the rocks of the coastline near the little villages of Brittany where she was born—her skin was splashed with the same reddish yellow color. Her features were softened by a mass of wild, sandy hair turning gray, which she tamed with a crimson ribbon. She wore a peacock blue and green tutu and white tights on her long, bony legs. Her singing voice was rich and dark, but her speaking voice was childish. With me she spoke the little bit of English she had learned from British trawler captains who fished near her village and flirted with her when she was a child. With my pitiful French we pretended to understand each other more than we did.

The North African children, who played in the streets without toys, but with never ending imagination, belonged to families who appeared and disappeared at random. Those energetic children seemed to find something amusing about me because they always put their hands on their faces and giggled when I smiled at them. But they crowded adoringly around Madame Clara when she appeared on the street with a smile and a tidbit or sweet for them.

Madame Clara was an ancient woman with an ashen, wrinkled face who wore long black dresses, and black shawls that covered her head. While the hurdy-gurdy woman stood out like a brilliant bird, Madame Clara seemed to blend with the setting. Gossip had it that she'd lived longer on the block than anyone else. It was also said that she was becoming senile and one day the pompiers would come for her and take her to a home for the impoverished aged. Only the children would miss her. The rest of us would hardly be aware that she was gone. Except that her apartment would be on the market.

Madame Clara's apartment was on the second floor of an ancient hotel on the other side of the street. It had been a famous brothel in the sixteenth century. I often saw her sitting near her window—a neighborhood watcher, a protector, a good angel to the children. Maybe she wasn't senile, just lonely, and needed someone to talk to. I made a mental note to do just that.

The other tenants in that building were the North African families. Some of the men were at times rowdy among themselves, but they were always respectful of Madame Clara.

On the morning after the murder, as I walked to the boulangerie on the cobbled street, trying to avoid what the pooper scooper machine had missed—which was practically all of it—I passed the clochard sleeping in his usual corner formed by one crumbling building jutting out in front of another. This morning he was lying in an embryonic position, one cheek showing, and as usual, cuddling an empty wine bottle. But something was different about him. He looked lumpier, as though he had more than a bottle in his arms. His face was cleaner and his stench wasn't so overpowering. He was wearing new running shoes. Maybe someone had given them to him, and then persuaded him to go to the shelter for a shower and shave.

I wondered, as I often did when seeing him like that, how he had gotten into such terrible shape. I wondered who he was when he used to be someone, before he was considered human garbage. Mostly he lay there in a drunken stupor when he wasn't dragging the wagon down the street, the kind of wagon that used to be attached to horses, not humans, making a terrible racket that punished our ears in our little fifth floor nest. The first time I looked down at him from our front window, I noticed how proud he seemed, pulling that heavy load, as though for that moment he thought he was someone. As I saw him straighten up, waiting for his pay, I foolishly thought the job meant a new life for him. I was wrong. It meant money for booze.

I shook off the image as I passed the shabby cafe halfway down the block. The shared tables set out on the sidewalk had a few unoccupied chairs and I had an impulse to sit down on one of them. I had been urging Sol to have breakfast there ever since we came. But he wouldn't. So now I did.

Among the people at the table was a man I never saw before, reading Le Figaro. I ordered my swallow of coffee from the North African waiter, and like an experienced New York subway rider, looked over my neighbor's shoulder, even though I couldn't read the French.

But I could understand photographs, and the picture I saw on the page gave me a jolt. It was Veronique's husband lying on the floor in their living room just as I had seen him. As I stared at the picture, I began to feel something was wrong, not exactly wrong, but something was missing. I closed my eyes and visualized the scene with the help of my mental camera. Then it came to me. The bronze statue of the naked woman wasn't there. And, unless it had rolled away out of range of the camera, neither was the wine bottle. I got a prickly sensation down my back.

As I stared at the picture, I could feel the man's eyes on me. I looked up from the newspaper. Those eyes were buried in a face like an upside-down pear, the expensive yellow kind. But a pear doesn't have bushy eyebrows or a sneering mouth. He was wearing a yellow shirt, an apple green tie, and a dark suit out of keeping with the neighborhood. Tacky anywhere. Click went my camera. The man handed me the newspaper as if my looking at it over his shoulder had dirtied it, then he got up and walked away.

I had been too interested in the newspaper to notice that someone else was now sitting across from me. It shouldn't have surprised me. She was always eating breakfast at this cafe when I went out for morning croissants. Breakfast? If you could call it that: a piece of bread and milky coffee.

She was my neighbor Sylvie whose television blasted until all hours from the building next door, beyond two sets of paper-thin walls. Sol and I had a to-do with her when we first moved in before I got to know her. Sol complained to the landlord about the noise and the landlord reluctantly inquired and found out that Sylvie had been through a crisis of the heart, as they say, and late night TV was how she coped.

When we asked him to tell her to cope more quietly, he gave us that Gallic shrug of the shoulders with the turned up hands that told us he would do nothing more. I could sympathize with the woman, but why should I suffer from her problems?

I'm a patient sort. I'd rather be inconvenienced temporarily, than make a big magilla out of things that can cause unpleasantness. So I endured the noise and waited for the opportunity to have a chat with her and work out a compromise.

The opportunity occurred on the night a movie was being shot in the street below, and the whole neighborhood, except for the all-night dress designer, was watching out the windows. A bunch of people with pads and pencils were scurrying around on the cobblestones, while, for no apparent reason, a skinny young woman ran up and down the street under a blinding shaft of light from a building across the way.

After watching for a while, I noticed someone on the balcony of the building next to mine. It turned out to be Sylvie of the blasting TV. She was leaning on the railing, her dyed blond hair tortured into a bun at the back of her head, and on her face the pallor and puffiness that comes from staying up late then getting up early to go to work. It must have been a pretty face before it was ravaged by who knows what. Wide, greenish eyes and a full red mouth brightened the drab setting. She was no longer a spring chicken. She was in that sad stage, between robust youth and robust old age, when suddenly your fresh, dewy petals wilt and your stem dries up and you know it won't be long before you become part of the good earth.

Her appearance and my knowledge of her lost love made me feel sorry for her. So one thing led to another and we had a friendly conversation and she invited me to tea.

At that tea, I got a little out of her about her "crise de coeur", as the French call it. She spoke more freely than she may have intended due to the liquid in her delicate Limoges cup—a dash of tea swimming in a sea brandy. Her English was pretty good, with a little fuzziness around the edges due to the tea.

Her lover, she told me, was younger than she, with a sensational prizefighter's body. She had given him her all and in return he had given her other women's lipstick stains to wash off his shirts. Not that she washed his clothes—she was a professional, you understand, working for a recording studio. For a long time she had suspected he was playing around, but when he fell under the spell of a younger woman, he abandoned her completely. He was obviously a bastard but even so she said she would never forget him.

So we compromised, as I had hoped. She still consoled herself with the TV, but at a lower decibel.

So there she was, the morning after the murder of Veronique's husband Jacques, sitting across from me outside the cafe. And she hadn't said a word. The North African waiter brought her usual without her asking.

"Good morning Sylvie. A friend of yours?" I pointed to the chair abandoned by the man with the upside down pear face.

"I never saw him before."

I knew by the look in her eyes and the way she dug her fingers into her bread that she was lying, but I didn't pursue it.

"Thank you for not playing your TV last night."

"The TV was off because I had an all-night recording session, not to please you."

"Well anyway, I was kept up until two from the dogs barking downstairs," I didn't mention what else kept me up, "but you can't have everything in life."

"Can't you? Tell me about it."

"Right. I guess life hasn't treated you too well," I said. "I never asked, but I always wondered, how come you speak such colloquial English."

"I should, I grew up on Long Island, and went to Hunter College."

"No kidding?"

"My parents were French and very wealthy. We came back to Paris when I was twenty. And here I am, suffocating in this crummy neighborhood."

It sounded like a cock and bull story. Why didn't I believe her? Maybe it was because her English didn't sound like from Long Island. It sounded like from the movies.

"Listen Sylvie. Could you read me what it says in the newspaper?"

She told me without even looking at it. "It says Veronique murdered Jacques. He deserved it. All men do."

"She murdered her husband?"

"Jacques wasn't her husband. He was mine. The dirty bastard."

I was at a loss for words. I thought of Jacques on the floor of Veronique's apartment. I couldn't visualize a prizefighter's body under that bloody leather jacket. But then again, she hadn't used the word husband about the man who had done her wrong—she had said lover. I visualized Jacques again, his bloody hair, and a pair of naked white feet I didn't remember seeing at the time. Or did I? The waiter came with my mouthful of coffee in a tiny cup. I guess he finally remembered me.

Sylvie wasn't so crazy about talking about her dead husband, because she got up and walked away, without even a "see you later," leaving almost a whole cup of milky coffee undrunk, and me with egg on my face, so to speak.

When I got back to the apartment with the croissants for Sol, there were two policemen waiting for me.

CHAPTER THREE

The two cops, Mutt and Jeff look-alikes, were wearing those cute uniforms you see riding around on bicycles in French movies. They saluted me. This was not the normal sort of behavior I witnessed among New York's finest. But I wasn't in New York.

"Bonjour Madame."

"Bonjour Monsieurs."

Silence.

I looked at Sol who was sitting stiffly in a put-together IKEA chair, definitely not his usual laid-back self. The two cops stood at attention like jelly apples on sticks with a transparent glaze over them. An atmosphere of quivering silence surrounded the three of them. If they came to see me, why weren't they talking to me?

"Sol, what are those cops hanging around here for anyway? What do they want?"

"How should I know?"

"You didn't ask?" He shrugged. Sol was adamant against learning French and reluctant to admit he understood what he understood.

"They must have said something."

"I'm sure they did. It's a matter of communication. They talk and I answer with a shrug. That they can understand. I got the impression they are waiting for their boss. That's all I can tell you."

Then he yelled at me in his quiet way. "Golda, why are you always getting us into trouble. Why can't you keep your nose out of somebody else's business for a change?"

"That's not fair! Never mind! What am I supposed to do, sit on my tush and watch somebody being murdered?"

"You poked your nose where it didn't belong and it didn't stop somebody from being murdered, so you might as well have stayed home in bed."

The two policemen looked away from us, embarrassed at the domestic growling. I followed their wandering eyes as they glanced at the yellowing window shades, at the brown, stained velvet wall covering, at the dark wood beamed ceiling hung with unreachable spider webs, at the dirty skylight above stairs with no handrail, at the two grimy little portholes that looked out at us from the bathroom on the balcony with the eyes of a giant vampire. Could this be the quaint wood-beamed apartment we had fallen in love with when we first saw It?

One of them took out a cigarette.

"Non, non!" I waggled my finger. He put the filthy weed back in its blue Gauloise packet with a disgusted sigh.

"Well, it wasn't Veronique that was murdered," I told Sol, "and from what I heard about her husband or whatever he is, he deserved it."

"What are you talking about?"

"Never mind!"

"Talk to them, you speak a little French."

"Little is right. Okay. Monsieur! Que voulez vous ici?"

What came out of his mouth was a bubbling stream of noise that sounded Italian. I was sorry I asked.

"Why didn't I think of it before? I'm calling Maxi, maybe I can get her before she goes to the studio," I said.

I looked at the big cop and gestured at the phone.

"Do you mind?" He shrugged. I dialed. The phone chirped. I caught Maxi before she left. She told me she would drive right over. She sounded grumpy.

My old school chum and dearest friend, Maxi, has lived in France for forty years, more or less. As a child, she never nurtured a dream to live in Paris like I did. But she had a rich father and after college, she came here on a whim. I had no visible father and stayed in America. I don't even know if she intended to settle here all those years ago—after the Second World War. But she did. Maxi lived in Paris in the springtime. Also in the summer, winter, and fall. She had love affairs that should rightly have been my love affairs, with famous artists. She painted in a studio that should have been mine. Finally, after a satisfying and spent youth she acquired a husband and kids and all that shit. I don't envy Maxi her Boris. He's not my type, though I am rather fond of him as Maxi's husband.

Me? What was I doing all this time? Me? The one with the dream of living in Paris? Sometime after World War II I married Sol, who was definitely my type, and we lived in a basement that had been a coal cellar. We survived on sardines and potatoes, which were all we could afford from what I earned painting eyes on ducks in a toy factory—and other such jobs—while Sol got his Ph.D. in Library Science at Columbia. When we finally emerged tattered and blinking into middle-class America, we had kids to think about—and Sol was immovable—no Paris for me when I was still young enough for its delights—or imagined delights.

Even when Maxi and I were kids she had it good. She lived on the Upper East Side with a maid and a cook and a Mama who didn't lift a finger, and slept till noon every day. I lived on the Lower East Side with a Baba to preside over me while Mama was destroying her health in a factory in Brooklyn that belonged to a rich cousin.

Do I sound jealous? You're damn right!

The bigger of the two policemen looked down his nose at me like I was a worm.

"Veronique didn't do it," I told him in my brand of French.

He shrugged again. In France, shrugging is a language in itself.

"What do you think you're doing?" Sol growled. "Trying to put yourself in jail?"

"All right, I'll shut up to please you, but I'll think what I want!"

Why were the Paris police butting into in my life? Were they harassing everyone in the building or only me? If so, what Nosey Parker told them I was snooping around in Veronique's apartment last night? Was it Sylvie? She could have. Her back window overlooked our courtyard. Did she see me running around in my nightgown? No, it couldn't have been Sylvie, she was at an all-night recording session. But then again, she could have been lying about that. I wouldn't put it past her.

So who was the real Sylvie? When she wasn't drowning in self-pity for a lost love, or bitter with hatred against men, or even people in general, she worked for this company that recorded famous pop singers I never heard of. That was her facade, but who was she on the inside? And by the way, who was that man sitting next to me at the cafe she pretended not to know?

I looked at the policemen who had invaded my privacy. They were standing by the window looking out. What was so interesting? I went to see. It was Madame Clara, with a shopping basket beside her on the cobblestones, handing out goodies to the street urchins. I hoped she wouldn't look up and see the policeman in my window. I decided to ask her up to tea the next time we passed in the street. Maybe she would tell me something about her life. I had never questioned my own mother, much to my regret. Maybe I could make up a little for this lack by learning about Madame Clara.

"I'm hungry," Sol said. "How about breakfast?"

I felt guilty. "I'm sorry, with all this mishmash, I forgot. I'll make coffee." Without asking permission from my keepers, I squeezed into the phone booth my landlord called a kitchen and turned on one of two working burners on the stove that occupied half the space. I made enough coffee for the policemen in case they wanted some. They wanted. At first taste they made sour faces, and handed back the cups.

"What's the matter, you don't like good American instant coffee?" I asked. They didn't understand, or pretended not to. Sol and I sat down at the table. I unwrapped the croissants au beurre. I had a second breakfast while we waited for Maxi.

It wasn't a long wait. Good old Maxi. You can always depend on her when you're in a spot. When she walked through the door those two French cops fell all over themselves. At her age she's still sexy. With Maxi it's always the same. Young French waiters who could almost be her grandchildren, flirt with her. She's not that beautiful. What does she have? Big brown eyes? Short blond hair out of a bottle? Maybe it's the way she carries herself, the way every schmatta she puts on those skinny bones becomes a designer dress. Who knows? Me? I never was sexy to men, not even in the first bloom of youth. Pretty I was, but too uncomfortable in my petals to attract the bees. So you can imagine, today at my age I didn't exist for those French cops as a desirable woman.

I explained the situation to Maxi—everything that had happened the night before.

She treated me to her most severe judgmental stare and let it set in before she asked, "Why are you always getting yourself into trouble, Goldie?"

"Why do you always sound like a broken record of Sol? Stop criticizing and ask those gorillas what they are doing in my apartment. They didn't even show me a warrant or whatever you need."

Maxie talked to the policemen, coyly—she couldn't help herself—it was second nature. They were like schoolboys, fidgeting at her attentions. Then she honored me with a glance.

"Goldie. Someone saw you going into the apartment. Don't worry, you are not a suspect. You won't be falsely accused. This is France." According to Maxi, everything in France is on the up and up while the rest of the world is corrupt. For her, France is the Garden of Eden before

Eve made the acquaintance of an apple. "The inspector speaks English so you didn't need to disrupt my life."

At that moment, the buzzer from downstairs startled us all. Sol answered it. The clumping sound on the outside stairs was followed by the plink of the doorbell. Sol opened the door to the inspector, the big Camembert cheese from the police department, who was gasping and clutching at his chest. He was followed by a notebook leading a cop. The big cheese breathlessly shook our hands and introduced himself as Inspector Hugues Potiron, while our two keepers stiffly saluted him. He was small. He had red hair. More red hair had migrated to his face. It was all surprisingly luxuriant. The light striking his glasses hid the color of his eyes. Sol and Maxi sat down on the couch to watch the performance in which I was to star.

Without ado, Inspector Potiron pulled two chairs from the table and arranged them so they faced each other. Then he gestured me to sit on one of them. I did. He took the other, jutting his face forward and radiating a benevolent, country-doctor smile that displaced a tuft of red cheek hair. I had to restrain myself from offering my wrist so he could take my pulse with his tiny delicate hand.

"Tell it me every people. I am happy English."

Alarmed, I looked at Maxi who had gotten up off the couch and was leaning languidly against the mini fireplace. She came to life, pulled a chair next to us and started chattering away to him in French. I understood enough to know she was telling him the story I had told her. I sat back and relaxed. What else could I do? Sol was now pacing the room and grumbling and stopping to scratch at the rash on his leg. The two policemen were looking out the window. The whole neighborhood could see them. It was embarrassing. The assistant was writing in his large notebook. In shorthand? I wondered.

Maxi stopped talking.

"Alors," said the big cheese. His face got so close I could smell his breakfast. "You are see a statue at scene murder? So big it is?"

"Maxi, for heaven's sakes!"

"Don't panic. Tell me what the statue looked like and I'll translate. This guy thinks he's God's gift to the English language."

"Okay, okay. It was bronze. Not so big. It was of a woman leaning down and washing her feet."

A lot of heated conversation followed.

Maxi looked irritated when she turned to me. "His French is almost incomprehensible. Some weird Southern dialect. Anyway, he says there was no statue when he got to the murder scene. He wants to know if you imagined it because you were upset at seeing a dead body. He even implied you are one of those Americans who make up stories for publicity."

"Tell him he's full of horseshit," said Sol, suddenly materializing in my vision.

"Take it easy, Sol, he's only doing his job," Maxi said.

Dearest Sol, I might have a few complaints about him now and then, but he will never let anyone push me around and he will never let me down.

"Listen, Maxi. Tell the inspector I saw what I saw, and if he doesn't believe me, it's his problem."

"I'll tell him you say the statue was definitely in the room when you were there."

"After that tell him he knows everything I know and it's time for him to leave, otherwise I will consider it harassment."

"Harassment? Listen Goldie, this is France not America. He wants to know if you can remember anything else."

"I can't. Ask him how someone could have seen me going into that apartment without being there themselves since there is only one apartment on each floor and the shade was down on the window facing the courtyard? Tell him the person he should be questioning is the person who ratted on me. That person could be the murderer. Tell him

Veronique could not possibly have murdered Jacques and tell them to stop accusing her to the newspapers."

"Are you crazy, Goldie? I'm not saying anything like that to the police. Ratted! You sound like one of your students!"

"Stop censoring me. Stop worrying about how I talk. You and Sol!"

"I'll simply tell them that you are positive you saw that statue. Okay?"

"You do that. Then after that ask who squealed on me."

"Jesus, Goldie!"

During that argument, Sol was quiet. He knew Maxi and I always fought about everything, so he wasn't alarmed. Maxi and I were friends in art school before Sol and I were even married.

So Maxi told the officers what she wanted to tell them and they bowed to her, shook hands and left. Good riddance.

"The Inspector said you probably won't be bothered again but not to go on any vacations before this thing is cleared up."

"I'm telling you Maxi, the person that saw me in the apartment could have murdered Jacques or at least knows something about it. If the police are not going to find out about it, I will. I'm not letting that sweet Veronique take the rap."

CHAPTER FOUR

After a night of trauma and a morning of Inspector Potiron, Sol decided to treat me to the modern art gallery at the Pompidou Center. He knows this is an oasis of peace for me—of wonderful paintings that can sooth away the rough edges of my angst.

To breathe in the heady aroma of Matisse and Rouault and Picasso is also to remind me once again that I could never have been a painter. I didn't have it in me. For me, striving for immortality is a fool's path— I mustn't regret what will never be.

I relaxed in the gallery and conversed silently with my friends on the walls. When my eyes began to close, I made for a comfortable fat chair under the tall windows and snoozed, while Sol walked slowly through the well-lit rooms and examined each painting.

When I woke up, I noticed the man with the upside down pear face disappearing into a far room. I had a moment of uneasiness then Sol was standing over me.

"If you wanted to sleep we might as well have stayed home and saved the entry fee."

"I like sleeping here."

Later, while we were eating supper, we gradually became aware of a rumpus in the street. Sol ignored it-something was always going on out there. But this time I wasn't so blase. I thought I'd better take a look.

Down below was a mob scene, waves of people splashed outward as though a stone had been dropped in a pool of humanity. In the center was a space surrounding two North African men throwing punches at each other. I knew them by sight—men who were usually chummy. But who knows what starts an argument among friends? Take Maxi and me—though we fight with words not fists.

I wasn't so interested in my food, so I stayed near the window and watched. In New York you wouldn't call those shenanigans a street fight. It was more like street theater. In New York fists would smash, not caress. In New York a knife or a gun could be involved.

The combatants looked like kids pretending, not really connecting, not really wanting to connect. I could see that for the onlookers, though, the combat looked real. The crowd was making angry noises as they focused on the men and egged them on.

"Goldie, come eat."

"In a minute."

I glanced at the corner where the clochard slept. He was still there in the exact fetal position as in the morning. Maybe he had gotten up, drunk his dinner then gone back to sleep in the same position. Then my view of him was blocked by the crowds.

When the crowds parted again, I could see the hurdy-gurdy woman in pants and sweat shirt. I almost didn't recognize her. If I didn't know better I would have thought she was a man. She disappeared into her building next door to the ancient hotel.

All up and down the street heads appeared in windows. Madame Clara was on her usual perch, watching. Tomorrow I will invite her to tea, I thought. Only the all-night designer, who was focused on cutting black cloth and attaching it to a dummy, seemed oblivious to the uproar in the street.

"Goldie, your food's getting cold."

"Okay, okay."

But I couldn't pull myself away. Things were heating up in the street. It was beginning to look like a real fight, a family feud, with men, women and children taking sides and encouraging their own. This made the two combatants cocky and they began to attack each other for real, landing hard punches that seemed to scare them. After hurting each other a little they allowed themselves to be pulled apart by their women. Separated, they gulped air and snarled at each other.

"Good evening Goldie." It was Sylvie on her balcony drinking a glass of champagne. She raised it to me. "Here's to the theater of the absurd."

I raised an imaginary glass to her. She downed the champagne and went inside, presumably for a refill.

I turned my attention to the street. It was between rounds. Two women were shouting at each other. Suddenly they began smashing each other with pocketbooks. Other women joined in. It began to look like an old Anna Magnani movie with the women connecting more fiercely than the men. Blood began to flow.

The two men, shamed by the ferocity of their women, jumped up and tried to separate them, which was difficult, because they kept getting hit in the face with pocketbooks. But they finally succeeded, and the women collapsed on the curb, while the men resumed their battle. This time all hell broke loose.

What were they fighting about? Who knows? It was a riot for the ears as well as the eyes, and people were now hooting from windows. I glanced at the clochard in his corner, barely visible through the mob. In a blur, I saw someone pull a large shopping bag out from under him. It all happened so fast that I wasn't sure what I saw—a baseball cap, a flash of face, a long coat, the figure quickly snaking through the crowd. A shopping bag? What could have been in it? Sol interrupted my thoughts.

"Come and eat, Goldie. Your food is getting cold."

"I'm coming."

Sol had missed the whole magilla.

I sat with him, I even picked up my fork, but I had no appetite for food.

Suddenly, above the noise of the mob, I heard police sirens and cars grinding down the block. Good, I thought, as I got up from the table, the show is over. Maybe the cops will bring peace then leave quickly. I had enough of cops for one day. I went to the window. Sol came and stood next to me. People were running in all directions. The police ignored them. I guess they were used to these happenings. Anyway, what did they care? Just a bunch of North Africans bashing each other. As long as they didn't attack the yuppies on the block.

Besides, they were busy elsewhere. They were standing over the clochard. Why? They usually ignored him. One of the cops moved just enough so that I could see him. He had been turned on his back, a cloth over his face. Was he dead? I heard a cry. It was coming from me. Sol put his arm around my shoulders and tried to pull me gently away.

"Don't look, Goldie." He was always protecting me against dead things in the street. Birds, pigeons, squirrels.

"It's alright Sol. I need to look." I wondered if the clochard had been dead when I had passed him that morning. My first thought was that the poor man wouldn't be pulling that wagon-load of folded boxes over the cobblestones making that terrible noise anymore. What monster could have killed this harmless, hopeless man? Even in France, the land of my dreams. I looked at Sol. The rash was creeping up under his chin.

We sat down at the table and studied our food. I was feeling uneasy, guilty.

"Solly."

"What?"

"There's something I forgot to tell Maxi when we were talking to the police."

"It's probably nothing. Please, Goldie, don't put us in deeper."

"It's not nothing."

"Alright tell them. You don't need my permission."

"It's just there was a wine bottle on the floor. What aggravates me is that Inspector Potiron doesn't believe me about that statue, so he won't believe about the bottle either."

"So don't tell him."

"But I saw it near the body and it was gone when the police arrived. At least it was not in the picture in the newspaper."

"So what will you do?"

"I'll think about it tomorrow."

CHAPTER FIVE

It usually hits you the day after the day after a sleepless night—the kind of fatigue that turns you into a zombie looking for its coffin. Actually it was more like two sleepless nights because the next night I couldn't get the picture of that dead clochard out of my head even though I tried to put it back into my files.

Sol was still asleep when I staggered out of bed. I heard voices and looked into the courtyard. Official looking people were still going into batiment B. I went down to the living room and looked out the front window. The clochard was not in his usual corner. Of course not! He was in the morgue. God, I was getting senile.

I had to resolve whether to tell the police about the wine bottle. I decided I should. I was sure it was important for them to know. But I'd need someone to translate. I dialed Maxi's number. Someone picked up.

"Maxi?"

"Damn, I knew I should have left ten minutes ago."

"I need your help."

"So what else is new?"

"I need your advice."

"You never take it."

"There's something I didn't tell the police."

"What's that?"

"I saw a wine bottle on the floor near the body. It wasn't in the picture in the newspapers."

"You got to be kidding. You're making a fuss about a wine bottle in France? I think the police have more important things to think about."

"I wouldn't bet on it."

"Maybe you're imagining you saw it."

"Maxi!"

"Goldie, I have to go."

"Listen, Maxi, there's something else, something I saw last night I didn't even tell Sol."

"Look, Goldie, stop letting your imagination run away with you."

I wanted to tell her about the person I saw taking a shopping bag from under the dead clochard, but what was the use? She wouldn't believe me. And maybe it had nothing to do with the case even though my intuition told me that the two deaths were connected, that the bag taken from under the clochard was important. It was just a gut feeling. I couldn't prove it, and I didn't even know what there was to prove. No point telling anyone about it. Especially not Maxi who doesn't believe anything I say anyway.

"My imagination is not running away with me even if you and the police don't believe me. The statue was there. I saw it, and it was bloody. It could have been the murder weapon. I think they should know about the bottle too."

"Stay out of it. It's not your business. The French police are very competent. They'll solve it without your help."

"I think I should tell them."

"Don't ask me to go with you. Don't expect me to interrupt my life to rush out and translate for you or bail you out of every mess you get yourself into. And while we're on the subject, you live in France and yet you are totally ignorant of the culture and language. You don't have a TV so you don't know what's going on, and you are not making an effort to learn the language!"

"Stop lecturing me! I could use your support, not your judgment. I can't go to the police by myself. Even if I was fluent in French I couldn't deal with that Inspector Potiron."

"Today is out. I have a doctor's appointment and after that a meeting at my gallery. I've got to go now, I'm late. We'll talk about it some other time."

Boris, her husband, is suddenly on the phone. She had the loudspeaker on, the fink. The last thing I wanted was to involve Boris in this. He has a way of screwing things up worse than I do.

"Goldie," he said, "Don't go to the police without talking to me first. Then if you have to, I'll go with you."

"Thanks Boris, you're a peach."

"I'll see you tomorrow."

"Tomorrow?"

"Don't you remember? We're going to Ecouen, that museum in a castle outside Paris, to see the David and Bathsheba tapestries."

"I'll pass it up. I already had Maxi's guided tour of the unicorn tapestries in the Cluny museum. They were stunning, but I didn't need her words to go with them. I like my visuals and verbals separate. When I want a story I go to a library not a museum."

"If you come, we can talk. Okay?"

"I'll come."

Sol was ecstatic about going to Ecouen. He loves that sort of thing-history and lectures. I also believe he secretly thought if he could get me out of Paris he could get me out of the pickle I had gotten myself into. I bet he was thinking if only I had taken a sleeping pill that night, the murder would have been just a ripple in our lives instead of a tidal wave. I was thinking if I hadn't shouted out the window when she was being strangled, maybe it would have been Veronique instead of her husband who was murdered. I had to stop thinking about it.

As I said, Sol was eager to see the David and Bathsheba tapestries in Ecouen. He is a Bible freak and can quote whole pages. Thank God he didn't memorize all the begats and recite them to me. Even so, when he starts quoting, I always wish I had a hearing aid to turn off.

Anyway I went to Ecouen because Boris said he would talk to me and I really needed to talk to someone who might believe me.

Let me introduce you to Boris. Maxi married him in her thirties, after she got tired of her wild, youthful exploits. I don't know if he was physically attractive then, but he isn't much to look at now—an aged Picasso satyr with scraggly white hair, pointed beard, ruddy cheeks, short stature and an eye for nubile women. He is Russian born and French bred-except for the war years he spent in New York. This was fortunate because, like Sol and Maxi and me, he is Jewish. I include Maxi even though her snooty parents didn't bother to tell her about her Jewish heritage until she was twenty, but that's another story.

Boris is a mad genius. He's many geniuses in one, mostly scientific but a little bit in the arts because his older sisters run a Russian-speaking theater in Montparnasse and he once put his foot into acting. He also speaks ten languages fluently. He also at one time worked in one of the French government departments. Doing what? I don't know. But his big love is his inventions and he spends every minute he can working on them. To each his own.

Since he's Russian as well as French, he's doing business behind the now shredded Iron Curtain. He's also taking his life in his hands making deals in that gangsterland called Russia, which he's always botching up. These deals are a heavy stone around Maxi's neck. The one deal he didn't botch up is something he's into with his sisters. He has a contract with a theater in Leningrad, excuse me, St. Petersburg to present French plays, like Moliere, and sometimes modern ones, translated for Russian audiences. To me, bringing theater to the land of Chekhov is like taking coals to Newcastle, but in St. Petersburg, it's considered chic to attend French plays. This is his only successful project. With Boris, to succeed in business doesn't mean to make a profit, it means not losing his shirt. So that's Boris.

I believe Maxi was besotted with him when they tied the knot even though she could have had almost anyone in Paris she wanted. She was besotted mostly because he is a genius and she considers herself a dummy which she hides very nicely by being judgmental of others. I believe it was she who ran after him. She didn't have to catch him, the turkey flew into her arms, even though he was always a skirt-chaser and still is.

They did the usual thing and had kids and so forth. But the lucky ducks had a maid to clean up after them, and a nanny to take the kids a few blocks to the Luxembourg Gardens to watch puppet shows while she painted in her studio and became modestly famous and continued her life of privilege.

Me? I took my kids to Riverside Park and sat around the sandbox listening to other mothers talk about formulas and potty training until I couldn't stand it any more and took a job watching other people's children grow up into a life of crime as a special ed teacher. So I didn't have a studio in Paris? Tough luck!

So the day after the day Veronique was murdered and the day after the clochard was murdered, I went to Ecouen because Boris said he would talk to me. But on that trip Boris and I never got the chance—and it turned out to be the worst day of my life.

CHAPTER SIX

I looked through the rear window of Maxi's car as we drove toward Ecouen. The face of the driver behind us seemed vaguely familiar, but it was too hazy to find in my mental files. Every time I looked back, there was that same face. When we changed lanes, so did the car behind us.

"We're being followed."

"Don't be silly, Goldie," Maxi said, putting on her distance glasses as the car made a little hop, "you're becoming paranoid."

Sol said, "We certainly are being followed—by half of the mishugana drivers in Paris. The other half of them are walking their dogs on rue Abbe Etienne."

Never mind the flippant remarks, I was positive we were being followed. That morning I had seen a car parked near the box depository. I didn't pay attention. And anyway, I'm not sure if it was the same car, but who knows? I turned around to take a mental photo of the man driving, but at that moment Maxi swerved into another lane too abruptly for him to follow. We lost him. So maybe I was wrong. I settled back and ignored Maxi's driving which always gives me the willies. How she and her passengers survived all these years was a wonder to me.

Boris said we'd talk when we went to Ecouen. Was there something he wanted to he tell me? Something about Veronique? Was she one of his old lovers? No, she couldn't have been. She was too young. So what was it? Boris was unusually quiet during the drive and I couldn't catch his eye. Maybe he didn't want to say anything in front of the others. Maybe it was just a trick to get me out of Paris.

The articles in the newspapers Sol had brought home implied that Veronique had murdered her husband—all lies—she was innocent. But where was she? Her disappearance could only add to the suspicions. Maybe Boris knew something. After all he'd once worked for the French government and had an inside track—and what he didn't know he had a knack of finding out.

Maxi parked the car near the castle that had been built for Anne de Montmorency and his wife, Madeleine de Savoie. That's right. His name was Anne. Don't ask me. I don't read guidebooks. I tried to listen to Maxi telling us why the architecture was revolutionary for its time. To me it looked just like every other French castle I had seen. Anyway I was there to see Boris not to listen to lectures. I moved toward him.

"Let's talk before we go in."

"Not now. I don't want Maxi to be suspicious."

Suspicious of what? I moved away from him, disgusted.

I had taken the trip for nothing!

Maxi was telling us that the castle had been built during the period of Henry the Second of Montmorency whose head was removed in 1632. I didn't catch the reason. Someone's head was always being removed throughout French history. At least it was a King Henry this time and not a King Louis. I still get the Louis mixed up. Anyway I wasn't in the mood for any more murders, even if they were historical. I was pissed off at Boris for luring me there on false pretenses, then abandoning me. I trailed after them, trying not to listen.

Inside was no better. Chock full of chotchkas, described in minute detail by Maxi who had been a tour guide when she first arrived in Paris. Too bad she never forgot any of it. The raison d'etre of the first drafty rooms were the elaborate friezes near the ceilings and huge fireplaces. I wished there were logs burning in them to warm us up; I wasn't dressed for winter in a castle. I was dressed for August in Paris.

Thank God we finally got to the tapestries where the whole scandal of David and Bathsheba was laid out in front of Sol's greedy eyes. He was in his milieu. He took over the lecture. He's usually a quiet man in company—a listener. Now he was spilling over with words and images. He didn't need a guidebook. He got it all from the horse's mouth, the Gideon Bible next to his side of the bed. Maxi let Sol talk, but she also let us know she's no slouch when it comes to tapestries and everything else in castles.

Me? I had enough talk. I took the imaginary batteries out of my imaginary hearing aid and straggled along at my own pace. I'm not interested in contents, only in the pleasure a work of art gives to the eye, as I said before. And those tapestries gave me a lot of that. Boris was ignoring the artwork and observing the slim legs of a guide enlightening a group of tourists.

It was then I noticed my one-time breakfast companion, the man with the face of an upside pear, among the tourists. Could he have been in the car that was following us? He wasn't driving, that was for sure. Was it a coincidence that he was here in Ecouen? This was possible. The most amazing coincidences happen in Paris. You are walking down an out-of-the-way street and you see someone you haven't seen in twenty years coming toward you. Anyway, the man went ahead of us into another room and I didn't see him again.

I looked at Boris. I could see that he had no intention of talking to me. He had lied to get me to come. Why? It was obvious an answer was not forthcoming. I had enough of that cold castle and I wanted to go home. But the others were enjoying their journey through history and who was I to spoil their pleasure? My head was beginning to throb and I longed for fresh air. So I whispered to Sol that I would take a little walk in the forest and be back soon. He was so engrossed in whatever he was looking at, I don't even know if he heard me.

So I went out.

That was the worst mistake of my life.

CHAPTER SEVEN

Outside in the clean, hot air of the parking lot, I couldn't wait to explore the forest near the castle. It felt good to be strolling alone—that is I thought I was alone, until I sensed a presence behind me. I started to turn and a hard body pressed against mine, a hand smashed into my mouth and a wet rag slapped my face. I gagged from the smell before passing out.

I woke up babbling and drooling in a stone grotto at the bottom of the ocean with eels swimming around me. The ocean water drained away and I'm sitting on a cold and slimy stone floor in a cellar—on rat droppings. I feel like vomiting. In front of me are two men on chairs with carved legs, wearing what the Brits call balaclavas over their faces. It's too dark to see their eyes through the slits, and I'm too dopey. There's a Tiffany lampshade covering the light bulb on the ceiling.

The men are talking in a language I don't understand. It doesn't sound like French or anything else for that matter, but in my condition my hearing could be faulty. I try to stand up to get away from the disgusting mess under me. I can't. I'm gradually aware that one of the men is talking to me in English in a heavy accent. I'm too muddled up to recognize it and I keep falling in and out of sleep.

"Are you awake, Madame?" The voice is insistent.

"Sometimes."

"You have only to answer one question."

"Ask and let me go home."

"Where is statue of Bathsheba?"

The word Bathsheba nudges me awake. Haven't I just been to see the tapestries of David and Bathsheba?

"Bathsheba is in Ecouen."

The other monster gets up from his chair comes over and hits me in the face. It hurts. I don't know anything else. I'm dreaming of bronze statues—the Degas ballet dancer in a gauze skirt, "The Thinker" in the garden of the Rodin museum, the smooth moon-like Brancusi "Bird in Flight."

And then I see the kitschy statue of a nude woman washing her feet in Veronique's apartment. Above it are blinking Christmas lights that spell out; "Bathsheba."

Lights are flashing in my face. My eye hurts.

I wake up vomiting. Very little of it lands on my clothes, thank God. I remember I'm wearing my second favorite Lord and Taylor outfit I bought just before I left New York. I wouldn't want anything bad to happen to it. I'm overcome by a sewery smell. I need to get out of here, but I can hardly move.

Then I remember Boris. He was the one who insisted I go to Ecouen. He was the one who told me not to talk to the police before I talk to him. Why? Is it Boris' face under one of the balaclavas? No. Both men are too big.

"Where is statue of Bathsheba?" The accent is now in place—definitely Russian. I am not too dazed to recognize it. And Boris is also Russian.

I hear myself answer. "What statue?"

"Madame. You know statue."

"I wish I did."

"You were there. You saw. Where is it?"

"Where is what?"

"Statue of naked woman."

Something clicked. He was talking about the statue I had seen in Veronique's apartment. "Was she washing her feet?"

"Yes. What did you do with it?"

"You think I'm strong enough to pick up a statue? Some mornings I'm too weak to pick up a cup of coffee." I hold out my trembling hand to show him.

"If you didn't take, who?"

"How should I know?"

First the police didn't believe there was a statue, and now these hoods think I stole it. Idiots all!

"Where is statue?"

"I told you I don't know."

I'm trying to figure out a way to knock him down and escape. My poor mind is going soft. In the best of times I'm no match for most men, and this moment is not the best of times. I am too weak to even stand up. The two of them confer while I try to remember the story of Bathsheba I wasn't listening to in Ecouen. Could the missing statue have something to do with the tapestries? Could the story of Bathsheba have something to do with the murders? My muddled mind gives me no answers.

The other man is getting ready to hit me again, I can see by the way he's kneading his palms. Who cares? So I'll dream of statues again. Better that than being awake, sitting on rat shit and taking abuse from human shits. I turn my face to the side so he can hit me on the cheek and not the nose. I have a beautiful classic nose that I don't want messed up.

I hear a woman scream. She is pleading in French I can almost understand. I think she's trying to save me from being hit again.

The man with the Russian accent is also speaking in French. I understand him because the words come out slowly. He is saying to the man who speaks with his fists:

"We made mistake. She knows nothing. If you hit her again you will kill her. I will not have blood on hands for this. We must let her go."

I was pleased to hear it. It's true, another smack like that would have put me away for good. In the movies people just get up and walk away from worse. Don't believe it. It's all lies.

The men go into a far corner to plan my fate.

"Madame…" I hear a weak voice.

Then I see a woman lying on the floor across the room. It's Veronique! She's alive! I have just enough strength to crawl on all fours to where she is.

"Arnaud…" she whispers to me, then puts her arms over her head.

I see the figure of the man with the fists loom above me, then a heavy shoe kicks Veronique's face.

I grab his leg with all my strength, then I feel a rag on my eyes. It's the same rag with the ether or whatever they put on my face to knock me out. I let go of the leg. I feel woozy and my eyes are burning. I close them tighter. I'm dragged up the stairs into a room with a familiar kind of smell. I'm too dopey to figure out what it is, and the camera in my mind does not photograph smells.

Footsteps. A hand mashes into my mouth. Then the footsteps fade away and a key is opening the door. I'm pulled outside into the heat, stumbling on cobblestones, slipping on something slimy, I don't want to know what. The cobblestones feel like the ones on rue Abbe Etienne. But that doesn't mean anything. All over Paris there are cobblestones.

What am I doing in Paris? I ask myself. How did I get myself into such a mess? I'm almost ready to go home to America—almost. It's a good thing Sol isn't here to read my mind. I'm shoved into a car—into the back with one of the goons.

We are bumping over Paris streets and I feel bruised all over and my eyes are sore. It's getting noisier from cars honking and screeching to a stop, and people laughing and shouting in the street. Am I someplace where life is normal, and people are doing the things normal people do-that I should be doing?

Through the schmatta on my eyes I see flashing city lights playing with shadows. I smell heavy gas fumes. My captors are shouting something at me. My face is smashed against the door. The door opens and I am flung out of the car. I am flung into howling traffic and suddenly the whole world is going crazy and lights are exploding.

CHAPTER EIGHT

I tear the rag off my eyes to a shattering attack of lights. I'm in the gutter and cars are honking at me and a bus is coming toward me. I crawl onto the sidewalk and sit there, blinded by auras of lights. I close my eyes and open them again to a familiar scene. I'm looking at the tourists at the cafe Aux Deux Magots. I wonder what they think about the free show I'm providing. Now they can go back home to America and tell their friends that Paris is just like New York. But I think they haven't even noticed me. They're too busy feeling special at a famous outdoor cafe sipping thimblefuls of coffee where famous writers put pen to paper in the nineteen twenties. They don't want to know about Paris bag ladies lying in the gutter. I pick myself up. A miracle I wasn't killed in that crazy Paris traffic. A miracle the light turned red after I was thrown out.

I looked down at myself. I was filthy. I crossed the street to the Church of St. Germain des Pres, the oldest in Paris, and one of my favorites. I thought about going inside and sitting down a while in one of the pews and savoring the peace. But the clochard on the steps blew me a kiss and I knew it was time to go home. So I passed the church by and went down the steps into the Metro.

Thank God that particular line was going in the direction of Clingnancourt, which meant I didn't have to change trains. Down on the platform people almost as grungy as I was were sleeping on the seats. Canned music was piped into the station like in a New York City elevator. But it was Monteverdi, not Montevani.

When the train came, I took one of those pop-up seats near the door. I looked around at the other passengers, wondering what they thought about me. They didn't even notice, and more than half of them were engrossed in paperbacks or journals. It did my teacher's heart good.

Someone better dressed than I was gave a spiel for money. All I understood was the word "voleur". He was probably asking us to give him money so he wouldn't have to steal it from us. He trundled down the aisle shoving his hand out to the other passengers, menacingly. Me, he ignored. He got off at Odeon and a kid playing the accordion got on and stayed on the train for a few stops while he went through his entire repertoire—two old songs.

The first was "Oh How We Danced On The Night We Were Wed," which always reminded me of my friend in high school who added the words, "If you think that we danced you've a hole in your head." The second number was "Bei Mir Bist Du Schoen," and it didn't sound like the Andrew Sisters. On my first encounter with one of those accordion players, I was so touched I parted with ten francs. The third time I knew I'd been had. I knew that somewhere in the depths of Paris was a Roumanian Fagan, you should excuse the anti-Semitism, who was providing a whole slew of refugees with accordions, and teaching them those two songs.

I got off the train at Etienne Marcel, crossed Boulevard Sebastopol and dragged myself toward home. I walked past the Russian art gallery on the first floor of our building. It was lit up, but I didn't bother to look in. Instead, I dawdled, examining my pilfered mailbox, prolonging the moment I would have to come face to face with Sol. But I had to go home. I painfully turned my key in the tall iron gate, leaned hard against it, and pushed it open.

With what was left of my energy, I took off my battered shoes and put them near the garbage bin next to a man's suit stained with something brown and walked upstairs in my tattered stockings.

The apartment had an empty smell, along with the usual odor of this part of Paris. Sol was not at home, for which I was thankful. It was already dark, but I had no idea of the time, or what day it was or how long I had been in that cellar. I took off my clothes and stuffed them in the garbage without a moment's sorrow for that expensive Lord and Taylor outfit. I wanted no reminders of the trauma in that horrible cellar as I walked up the stairs to the bathroom on the balcony, not caring that the all-night dress designer could see my naked bruised old body through the window if he happened to be looking.

I filled the ancient bathtub and soaked in hot water that slowly turned gray. I felt myself relaxing into sleep. I didn't fight it. I woke up with my chin under water—drowning would have been an anticlimax.

I tried to stay awake by conversing with myself about inanities like, "Why me God?" and remembering when a tough, street-wise kid brought a butterfly to school in a jar and wept because it couldn't fly when he set it free. I shampooed my hair and rinsed it with the hand-held shower. As the swampy water slowly oozed down the drain, I stood up and rinsed the dirt and soap off my ancient body. I lusted after a good old-fashioned American shower with endless hot water and a curtain to keep it from spraying the moldy carpet. But I was happy enough with what I had.

Dry and in a bathrobe, I looked in the mirror. A mouse was nibbling at my eye. Oh well, if that was the worst of it. I looked through the porthole that overlooked the living room, and out the front window. I could see the all-night designer cutting fabric. Now that I was feeling a little better, I was embarrassed that he might have seen me in the street looking like a bag lady. I don't know why I felt that way. I had seen him once or twice in more compromising situations. Not with women, but with men. But anyway, a little romance is not comparable to my situation.

The door slammed. I heard voices and felt comforted by them. I heard the happy yelp of Sol as he ran up the stairs, came in the bathroom and hugged me.

"You're home. Goldilocks! How did you get here before we did? We almost called the police."

Then I knew it was still today in spite of everything that had happened.

"I'll tell you about it when we go downstairs. I have to sit down and unwind a little."

His voice became scolding. "We spent hours looking for you in the forest. What happened?"

"Give me a chance…"

Maxi poked her head in and made a "tsk" sound. "You're behaving like a child. You're lucky Boris suggested we come here and see if you were back before we called the police."

"You're right. I had enough police for a lifetime."

So why didn't Boris want to call the police? What didn't he want them to know?

CHAPTER NINE

The four of us were having a little drink—a little vodka I kept in the closet for Boris. There wasn't any food in the fridge, and even if there was, I wasn't about to prepare a meal.

"I know a restaurant in the neighborhood that's not too expensive," Maxi said.

"Not yet. I still have to recover a little." Actually the thought of food made me nauseous.

"Of course. Eating before nine is barbaric," Maxi said.

I looked at the clock. It was after nine.

"Maxi is more French than the French," said Boris.

I looked at him in a different light. In just a few hours he had become a stranger to me. He had tricked me into going to Ecouen. Why? Was he feeding me to those goons who kidnapped me? I would have to be careful what I said in front of him.

"How did you get that mouse, Goldie," Sol asked me.

"I fell over a rotten tree stump while I was walking in the woods near Ecouen. You know me, if it's there I'll trip over it." Nobody laughed. Why did I lie? I blushed with guilt.

"We looked for you all over those God-damned woods. How come we didn't see you if you were falling over stumps?"

"I got lost. I was lost for a long time until a nice man found me and took me back to the castle."

Boris didn't say anything. His behavior had been suspicious since the day before when he asked me not to contact the police. And there were other odd happenings, like Maxi's car being followed, and the pear-faced man popping up in the museum. Was he involved in my abduction? Was Boris? I only knew I couldn't trust him anymore. Too bad. I could trust Maxi with my life, and Boris was Maxi's husband.

"So did this person who found you drive you home?" said Sol asking me a question and providing me with an answer at the same time.

"Yeah, I bummed a ride."

"How convenient," Boris said. There was a funny look in his eye. Who was he really? After so many years, I needed to know more than the obvious things, the things that reinforced the image he wanted to create. Who was the man inside him? How could I find out without making him suspicious? I could ask him seemingly innocent questions. Even though I was feeling lousy, and the sewery smell of the cellar kept backing up on me like an undigested pizza, I turned to him.

"How come you and Maxi got together? You two are like oil and water."

"Oil and vinegar is more like it. When we are in the same bottle we shake it up. Why do you ask?"

Maxi snorted and raised her eyes to the ceiling.

"You didn't answer my question, Boris."

"I'll answer. Maxi was the sexiest thing that came to Paris after the war. I was a funny looking little schlemiel and didn't have a chance with her. But I never gave up. I waited around until she used up all the handsome guys."

"Don't be so modest, Boris. Women always found you sexy—not me of course—but you had all the women you wanted." I started to say you still do, but I didn't want to hurt Maxi who was already looking uncomfortable.

The innocent question routine wasn't working. I wasn't going to learn anything relevant because I couldn't ask the kind of questions or get the kind of answers I needed in front of the others.

"Listen," I said, "Boris and I have something to talk about. We'll go upstairs to the bedroom."

"Good," said Maxi. "I always told you if you want to learn French, take a French lover like I did."

"Don't talk dirty in front of Sol, Maxi. You sit there and flirt with him and think about what you want to order in that nice restaurant you told us about. Boris and I won't be long."

Upstairs, we sat on opposite sides of the bed under that Paris roof. I positioned him so he could just see Veronique's window even though the shade was pulled down. I thought it would give me a psychological advantage—in case he was involved in Jacques' death. I almost expected Veronique to pull up the shade and wave at me. But she couldn't, could she? She was elsewhere, in a rat-infested cellar.

With the heat pushing in on us from all sides I remembered how cold I had been in that cellar. I was sure now that Boris had something to do with my being there—and that he could rescue Veronique from those goons, if he wished. Yet somehow, being alone with him, looking into his face, he didn't look so menacing. A part of me couldn't believe he was involved in something so sinister. I looked at him, trying to figure out how I could question him without forcing him to retreat, or lie to me.

"Boris, you insisted I go with you to Ecouen so we could talk. But we didn't talk, did we? Now we can. What did you want to say to me?"

"I don't remember."

"Baloney!"

We were looking at each other, me with fire in my eyes.

"What really happened to you in Ecouen, Goldie."

"You tell me, Boris!"

"How should I know? I was with the others."

"Don't give me that rubbish. I'm not afraid of you."

"My God, why should you be afraid of me?"

"You wanted to get me out of Paris, didn't you?"

"Yes."

"Aha! Why? Was it because you were afraid I might go to the police?"

"I was afraid the police might go to you."

"Why? What are you involved in?"

"I can't tell you yet."

"You are keeping secrets from me?" I was outraged. "If I hadn't gone to Ecouen on your suggestion, I would have been spared all that horror."

"What horror?"

I hadn't intended to show my hand, but I was so angry with him I couldn't restrain my mouth. But what difference did it make? If he was involved he already knew about it. And if he wasn't, well then maybe I was too hasty in my judgment of him.

I regurgitated what had happened to me in the parking lot in Ecouen—and the rest of it. To my surprise, a cloud of pain replaced his usual pixie-like expression, but he didn't seem surprised. What was I to make of that? Was I right to believe he was mixed up in Jacques' murder? Looking at the pain in his face I suddenly had doubts. No matter what it cost I had to find out what was going on with him.

He nodded toward Veronique's window. "I want you to tell me what you know about that statue of Bathsheba you told Maxi you saw."

How did he know the statue was called Bathsheba? I hadn't mentioned that to Maxi. I only knew the name because that's what the thugs in the cellar called it. And why was everyone so interested in the statue? Those schmucks who kidnapped Veronique, the police in a negative way, and now Boris. A statue called Bathsheba? A piece of crap like that doesn't deserve a name!

I breathed in deeply. "How do you know the name of the statue?"

He looked evasive. "I have connections and I used them when I heard you were involved."

"Hmph. Government connections?"

"Sure. Government and others."

"Underworld?"

"Underworld."

Right. So now he was admitting he was somehow mixed up in this affair. But how? Was it peripheral, innocent? Maybe he was just acquainted with the criminals, but wasn't one himself. Or maybe it was true, he was only interested because I'm a friend of Maxi's and I'm involved. But that's baloney.

I was exhausted. I had enough trauma for one day and besides if he had something to do with murder, which at that moment I didn't want to believe, he wasn't about to tell me. And anyway, my head wasn't working well enough to catch him unawares.

"Goldie, you have to be straight with me about that statue."

"I told you everything I know. Why don't you talk to the Police?"

"They don't believe it exists. You know that. Goldie, you are holding out on me."

"Who me?"

It's true. I was. I didn't tell him I had seen someone grab a shopping bag from under the clochard who was lying dead on the street. I didn't tell him because I didn't know if I could trust him—didn't know if he was lying to me. I only knew that at that moment, the look on his face changed from the kind expression I had known for so many years into an almost sinister grimace under the dim light of the uncovered bulb hanging from the ceiling—a bulb too much like the one in the cellar. I thought idiotically that I ought to buy a Tiffany shade for it.

"Okay." His eyes became soft again. "I won't push you now. I'm sorry you got mixed up in this." He took my hand and squeezed it warmly. I withdrew my hand, I wasn't going to let him hype me.

"Wait a minute, Boris, tell me what you know about Veronique."

He hesitated. "She was a famous model who started posing when she was hardly out of diapers. She became a later-day Kiki of Montparnasse, a darling of artists and writers. She posed for late Picassos, was photographed by Man Ray. Then she went out of style and on the skids. Goldie, did she say anything to you in that cellar? Anything about that statue?"

It was my turn to hesitate. "Not about the statue. She said 'Arnaud' that's all."

"Arnaud? He's her former lover, the crook and gigolo who owned the gallery across the street until he disappeared. It became some kind of factory after that."

"The box depository?"

"Maybe."

"What do you mean, 'disappeared?' "

"Nobody's seen Arnaud for years. No one knows why or where he went. He had a long-term hot affair with Veronique, and a passionate breakup."

I was trying to digest this information when Boris said, "I know you're holding something back. But after what you've been through today, I won't lean on you. Just let me know when you're ready to tell me about it, okay?"

"Why is this statue so important to you Boris?"

"I can't tell you just yet."

"Right. If you have nothing else to say, I'm hungry." I wasn't, I was getting jumpy and claustrophobic in that hot airless room with Boris.

CHAPTER TEN

I'm a light sleeper, and I was awakened in the wee hours by a steady dripping sound. I found the cause right away, a leak from the toilet tank. The rug in the toilet room was sopping wet. I didn't want to be blamed for a deluge in the living room, or the apartment below—the howling dogs wouldn't appreciate that. It took great physical prowess to awaken Sol. He didn't thank me as we emptied buckets till eight in the morning. This I didn't need after the day I had. We called our landlord and asked him to send a plumber.

Let me introduce our landlord. Monsieur laid-back-pudgy, balding, aging young actor who was still living on the glory of a bit part in a Belmondo movie. For years after that he haunted Hollywood for his big break, then slunk back to Paris to offer us his moth-eaten and moldy Garden of Eden while he retired to his ancestral home in a suburb on the banks of the Seine.

We rented the apartment after his sincere avowal that it was quiet. Quiet? Sounds of rock bands thumped their way through the night from apartments facing street and courtyard. Later, when we finally gave notice, he tried to convince us to stay by offering us leftover earplugs he no longer needed in the quietude of his country home.

"My plumber is on vacation," a sleepy voice said.

"What should we do? The apartment is in danger of a flood."

"Get a plumber."

"What plumber?"

"Any plumber. Ask the real estate agent who rented the apartment to you. I'm very busy."

"Busy sleeping," I grumped at Sol. Sweet, angelic Sol was spending part of his involuntary exile at the English library a few blocks away in the Pompidou Center, researching a book he has yet to finish on a subject so esoteric no one would read it if he did. What the subject was I never found out. On the day of the deluge he stayed home, his rash peeping out above his collar.

"Sol," tell me again the story about David and Bathsheba," I said as I went up the slippery stairs—slippery because our landlord's maid had waxed and polished them diligently to make an impression on us before we moved in. I poured out a bucket of water. The speed of the drip was accelerating. I went downstairs.

"I told you the story at Ecouen," he said.

I hated to bother him. I knew his mind was far away on his book, or his grandchildren, or who would win the playoffs. But I had to know.

"You told me, but I wasn't listening. Please tell it again. I think it might have something to do with my ordeal."

"What ordeal?"

I suddenly remembered that Sol knew nothing about what I had been through the day before—because I deliberately hadn't told him. It was the first time in our life of togetherness that I kept something big from him. I didn't feel good about it.

"You know, the murders—Jacques and the clochard."

"I thought we were finished with all that. But I'll tell you the story."

Between emptying buckets of water and waiting for the plumber sent by the real estate agent, I listened in fascination. This is the gist of the story.

During some kind of biblical war, King David sent his general, Joab, to the front to fight while he stayed home for some unexplained reason. One evening the king got out of bed and walked on his roof. He looked down over the parapet and saw this beautiful woman. He was smitten. What else? When he asked who she was, he was told she was Bathsheba the wife of Uriah, who was fighting for him in the war. So King David sent for her and slept with her, that creep. I suppose she was willing, so they couldn't call it rape. Today they might. Anyway the next morning he sent her home.

Naturally she got pregnant after that one time, like they always do in fiction. She told King David about it. He sent for Uriah and told him to go home and wash his feet, which may have been code for "sleep with your wife so people will think the kid is yours." Well, Uriah didn't. He slept outside the palace with the servants. When the king asked him why, he said he couldn't enjoy the comforts of life and wife while his buddies were sleeping rough in the fields.

So David tried again. He fed Uriah, made him drunk and sent him home. Again Uriah didn't go. So I guess David gave up, because the next day, he gave Uriah a letter to take to Joab at the front which said that the general should send Uriah into the arms of the enemy then leave him there to die. Which Joab did. King David was then free to marry Bathsheba, and after a little this and that, they ended up with a son who became wise king Solomon.

That story was woven into ten tapestries in Ecouen. Did this story parallel the case I had gotten myself mixed up with? If so, Veronique was Bathsheba and Jacques was Uriah. But who was King David?

My own King Solomon is also wise. Maybe I should have told him what was going on. But I didn't. The less he knew the better. For his own safety.

The plumber finally arrived. No English at all, of course. Happily, my French was adequate for the situation and when it wasn't I used hand-pictures. He informed me that the problem with the tank was fairly simple. It dripped because a certain doohickey was so ancient and rotted it no longer worked and needed replacing—a fifteen minute task.

"Our proprietaire will be pleased to hear it," I told him. The plumber was a husky man with a pleasant rumpled face and the winey aroma plumbers carry around with them all over the world.

He told me, "It's good I am here, so it will be done today before the whole system explodes. But first I must turn off the robinet (tap) under the toilet to avoid flooding."

I remember distinctly he used the word "explode,"

Because I looked it up.Unfortunately the robinet was too rusted to turn off, so the plumber searched the apartment for the central tap. He couldn't find it.

While all this was going on, Sol was sitting in a patch of sun in the living room, reading. When I told him what was happening, he looked at me with glazed eyes.

"Go to the library, Sol. I can handle this."

"You sure?"

"The plumber's no King David and I'm no Bathsheba."

He left and I called the proprietaire.

"Tell the stupid man the robinet is under the kitchen sink." I could hear the yawn in his voice.

And so it was—also too rotted to turn off. The entire water system in the building would have to be shut down so that the plumber could do the fifteen minute chore in the tank of the toilet. But where was the central robinet? Such a pretty word-robinet. I thought I could hear it chirping.

"Oh la la!," said the plumber.

And so the search began.

"The robinet must be in the cellar," he said, "but where is the cellar?"

I called the proprietaire and asked where the central robinet was located.

"How should I know? Such things never happened when I lived there. Call the agent."

"If you don't know, why should she?"

She didn't.

We rang doorbells. It was a mystery to everyone. The hours were passing. The plumber was costing whatever Paris plumbers cost. It was not my problem, I thought, except I was losing the entire day. I had already lost a night's sleep over it. The policeman guarding batiment B must have thought we were mad, but he said nothing.

On one of my trips down the stairs, I met one of the two-legged occupants who lived with the dogs below us. She wore a leather miniskirt and a thick layer of make up to cover her emerging wrinkles.

"I'm sorry to disturb you," I managed to say in French, "but would you please try to do something about your dogs barking at night."

"It is not my dog."

"Not your dog?"

"My dog never barks when I am away. Mais non! Jamais!"

A remarkable woman. She could hear her dog not barking from the restaurant where she worked.

"And the dog of my friend also does not bark. It is the dog beneath us that barks. I also have heard him."

"And does he yelp to greet you in two voices when you get home at two in the morning?" I couldn't manage all that in French so I said it in English.

She turned up her nose and started to walk down the stairs.

"Excuse me, do you know where the robinet for the building is?"

"Telephone the manager."

"What's the name," I shouted down to her.

"Robinson," she shouted up and I heard the gate slam.

I ran upstairs again and found the Robinson agency in the telephone book. The robinet was in the basement under the Russian art gallery on the ground floor. The gallery was out of business, but the plumber could pick up the key at 4:30. The plumber left for lunch. God forbid a Frenchman should miss his midday feast.

I explained the situation to Sol over a salad.

He took it philosophically. During the pause from the plumbing crisis, I thought about the cellar I had shared with Veronique and the rats. I desperately wanted to pour my heart out to Sol, explain the mess I was in, my suspicions about Boris—and be comforted by him. But I didn't, the less he knew the better.

Sol was in a hurry to get back to work, so I decided to walk with him to the Pompidou Center. Downstairs, just before we got to the gate, I saw two men coming out of the Russian art gallery. I froze. One of them was Boris, the other was a stranger. Then they were gone.

"Wasn't that Boris?" Sol asked.

"I don't think so. What would Boris be doing here?" I hated lying to him so much.

"I thought the key wasn't available until four thirty."

"I thought so too. Anyway. It's not us paying the bill."

At four-thirty, the plumber arrived in a mist of wine and garlic. He unlocked the gallery and we went in.

The odor was of old canvas and paint, and dust—the same smell that had hit me when I was dragged up from the cellar. I was tumbling into the past—the rag wet with ether on my face—I was going under.

"Madame?" I felt a reassuring pressure on my arm. I opened my eyes and breathed deeply. The smell of ether was gone.

"Madame?"

"It's nothing, let's go down to the cellar."

I was afraid of what I would find. But I had to go. I had to know for sure.

I forced myself down the steps. I forced myself to enter that room of terrible memories, fearful of what I'd find. Thank God Veronique was gone. What remained was water oozing from the walls and two antique chairs soggy with damp. I hoped Veronique was safe wherever she was. But I had a sinking feeling.

The plumber seemed to notice only the complicated nest of water pipes and the working robinet. He fiddled around with it while I digested the knowledge that I had been a prisoner in the basement of my own building, before my captors had put me in a car and dumped me on Boulevard St.Germain-des-Pres across the Seine.

When the water was turned off we went upstairs and outside. I was happy to breathe in the swampy air of the Marais. Sol was waiting for me in the apartment. He had brought me a treat. All kinds of pate and celery root salad and a nice red wine for dinner. But at the moment, dinner was still a long way off.

I went up to the toilet room with the plumber and watched as he worked. The doohickey in the tank was replaced in fifteen minutes, just as he had predicted. When the water was turned on again, I heard a loud, gurgling sound as filthy water shot up from the drains like the fountains of Versailles. The plumber, by now my pal, said he would clean the drains for us free of charge and then poured in a large container of acid. With loud glugging and sucking sounds, the brackish water in the sink and bathtub disappeared down the now unclogged drains.

It was time for the reckoning. The cost of the replacement of the doohickey wasn't much, but a day's wages was astronomical. He presented us with a bill for a day in the life of a plumber.

"Send it to the landlord."

"No way!" or the French equivalent. I guess he knew the type he was dealing with. He wanted his money up front, or else we'd have a resident plumber.

I phoned the landlord. The phone almost melted when he heard the charges.

"The man's a crook!" Takes one to know one, I thought.

"Take it up with the crook," I said, handing the phone to the plumber. A lot of angry Gallic sputtering filled the air. Sol went into the den and closed the door. The plumber handed me the phone.

"He's a liar and a cheat," the landlord growled. "but if you pay him by cash, the bill will be less, because he won't have to pay the tax."

"Me? I'll only pay if you promise to reimburse us. Better still, I'll deduct it from next month's rent."

"Yes, yes. I'm very busy."

He kept his promise. Unfortunately we weren't compensated for the sleepless night and stressful day running up and down the stairs and worrying about water explosions. Anyway, except for the trip to the cellar, it took my mind off the murders, and my worry over Veronique.

When I had time to think about something besides exploding toilet tanks, I was determined to find out why Boris had been in the Russian gallery. My suspicions about him were gnawing at me again. Where did he get the key? What was he not telling me? Was it possible that Boris was King David?

I impulsively called him.

Boris was in his workshop, Maxi told me—inventing something useless, I was sure. She'd see if he was available. Boris calls his cockamamie creations his children, and even has patents on some of them. But no manufacturer has offered to put money into them. Boris is obsessed not only with his "children," but with making enough money to finance them himself. Hence his business trips to Russia.

What are these inventions? Who knows? Some kind of electronic thingamabobs. I actually saw one once. It was little and squiggly. He told me what it was supposed to do, but Boris doesn't always make himself clear. Maybe, just maybe, it was all a smokescreen for something more sinister.

Maxi picked up the phone and informed me that her husband was too busy to talk to me. Oh well, if he was King David, he wouldn't tell me about it. He would probably deny what I saw with my own eyes, that he was in the Russian gallery that afternoon.

When I put down the phone, Sol said to me, "Goldie, You look very tense. I want you to enjoy the supper I bought, so let's go for a walk first."

It was true. I was wound up tight like a ball of wire. And I was exhausted. Sometimes walking rejuvenated me, mentally and physically. "Okay. A short walk. As far as your beloved Notre Dame."

CHAPTER ELEVEN

As Sol and I strolled down rue Abbe Etienne, my muscles began to unkink. Near the Pompidou Center I caught sight of the man with the upside down pear face. He was pretending to look at a newspaper at the kiosk. Maybe he lived in the neighborhood, but that didn't explain why he was at Ecouen, why he was always hanging around. It couldn't be coincidence. It was just another thing I had to take up with Boris.

"Goldilocks, relax. When we get home I'll give you a backrub." That sounded nice.

"I'll try."

As I trundled past the Pompidou Center I glanced at the street circus in the concrete basin near the entrance—the strong man, the fire-eater, the guitar player and the artist who drew portraits of tourists—this colorful vision of Paris gave a wry flavor to my angst.

We passed the Stravinsky Fountain with its delicate, metal tracery, its moving wheels and hoses expelling flutes of water—and a bulbous creature in primary colors, with a seven finger gold hat. Huge red lips blew kisses. A snake twined and hissed. Tinguely constructions married to Nikki de St. Phalle sculptures.

As I walked over the Pont d' Arcole hanging onto Sol, the mood of the sky changed without warning as it often does in Paris. Clouds crept over splotches of blue sky until a gray dripping sponge hung over the Ile de La Cite. By the time we had crossed the bridge, great hands of rain were slapping us.

We splashed into the nearest bistrot where we dripped and shivered and I had a sudden yen for a nice cup of hot tea and toast. We made for a free table in the back with a curved banquette, squeezed in, and cuddled for warmth. The cafe soon filled up with other wet people, including a young couple at a table cozily near ours.

Through the window I could see the hurdy-gurdy woman in a doorway trying unsuccessfully to keep her instrument dry. I guess for once her weather predictions went wrong, else why was she caught in the rain like the rest of us fools? She suddenly made a leap for the door and entered, taking the one remaining seat near the window. The scarlet bow in her hair drooped. With her sandy hair flat against her head, she looked like a man in drag. I waved. She winked and blew me a kiss.

A country-type waiter distracted me as he approached and handed Sol a menu. He wasn't the usual bistrot waiter who sneers down at you and couldn't care less whether you order or not. He had the look of a barnyard creature stuffed into a tuxedo. His mane of ginger hair was unkempt, and his eyes reflected the sky. Sol ordered a cafe express. I ordered tea and buttered toast. The waiter, looking dazed and lonely in the big city, walked away. Snug and warm now, we watched the rain descending beyond the hurdy gurdy woman, beyond the plate glass window. My mind was gloriously empty when my food arrived—two skinny frankfurters. No toast, no tea. Sol got his cafe express, though.

I handed back the plate and patiently showed the waiter my choice on the menu. He blinked and retired to the kitchen. I eagerly awaited his next offering. When it finally came, toast was at least part of it—a Croque Monsieur—toasted ham and cheese.

"Non," I said, and patiently explained again what I wanted.

He hunched his shoulders and left. On his next appearance he got it right—dry toast, a pot of jam, and a pot of tea. Voila!

But that wasn't the end of it. As I bit into my toast and sipped my tea, the young man sitting at the next table was presented with what looked like the very same croque Monsieur I had rejected.

He picked up his knife and fork and started to cut it. He couldn't. He hacked at it—but didn't make a dent. He was a determined young man and finally separated a chunk. The orange surface gleamed as he delivered it to his mouth. Then he started to chew and a startled look came over his face. He seemed to have difficulty ungluing his teeth. His woman, intrigued, asked for a piece, which he managed to sever for her. She chewed endlessly. They looked at each other. She giggled. He shoved the plate away and put a napkin to his mouth.

I started to laugh, so did the people at the tables around us who had been watching the pantomime, and so did the young couple. The sun, curious about all the mirth in the bistrot, suddenly looked through the plate glass window and smiled. The chair where the hurdy-gurdy woman had been sitting was empty.

The laughter was good for me. I needed all the laughs I could get to deal with what was waiting for me when I got home.

CHAPTER TWELVE

Boris, leaning against our building, stood at attention as we approached. It was my chance to have it out with him. to find out if he was the new and sinister Boris I had glimpsed the night before—or the kind, generous Boris I had always known. But I was torn. I knew Sol wanted a quiet dinner with me, and then bed, after a sleepless night trying to prevent a deluge in our apartment. Maybe I could have both.

"You are just in time for dinner. Sol brought home a feast."

"No, thanks. I have to talk to you alone, Goldie."

I turned to Sol, "As you may have gathered, Boris and I have taken Maxi's advice. We're having an affair, do you mind?"

Sol shrugged. He was getting very French in spite of himself. "Enjoy, it's human nature."

What does Sol know about human nature, forty years a librarian at Columbia University?

"Let's take a walk, Goldie," Boris said.

"Solly, do you trust Boris?"

"What do you mean by trust."

"I mean—I would trust Maxi with my life," I told him.

"I trust you to take a very short walk with him while I put the food on the table."

That didn't answer my question. But only Boris could allay my doubts.

"We can go to that cafe down the block."

"I've had enough cafes, thank you, let's get this over with", I said.

Boris took my arm roughly and walked me down the block as Sol disappeared into the entrance of our building.

The clouds had scattered as quickly as they had gathered. The sky was now soft and hazy the way Paris skies get after the rain when the sun is slipping away. It's a painter's light, Maxi always says. She should know. As we walked I felt eyes peering out from windows.

I saw Madame Clara looking down at me. Was she keeping an eye on me, along with the children playing in the street? If so, why? Did she think I was in trouble and wanted to spread her protective cloak over me? I dismissed the thought. I hoped she hadn't seen me in my incarnation as bag-lady, but I wouldn't bet on it.

Up ahead, the hurdy-gurdy woman had dried out and was serenading us with a Breton song. Her voice sounded hoarse, almost like a man's. Boris didn't seem to notice.

I was, at the moment, feeling a bit suspicious of him, but as I glanced at his profile, I could see by his expression that something was very wrong. Perhaps he would tell me about it. I didn't think he would, but I chanced it.

"Are you in trouble?" I asked him.

"Yes."

"What is it?"

"I might tell you. But first you have to be straight with me. I know you're keeping something from me. I need to know what it is."

I was. I decided to keep it from him a little longer and tell him my theory instead. I'd be straight with him when he stopped being crooked with me.

"I believe there's a Bathsheba-King David connection. I believe Veronique is Bathsheba and the clochard, who was found dead on our block, was the agent of David, whoever he is. I believe the clochard killed Jacques, like Joab killed Uriah-more or less. The big question is: who is David?"

"You're talking nonsense. That's not what I came to hear."

"I still believe the clochard killed Jacques."

"What evidence do you have for that?"

"Gut feeling." I had more than that. But he still hadn't said anything to make me trust him.

"Forget about the clochard. Forget that King David nonsense. Did you see anything out of the ordinary in Veronique's living room when you found the body?"

"Only the statue. And a wine bottle on the floor. That clochard is a wino."

"A lot of them are. Goldie, you're not telling me anything. I have to know more, or…"

"Or what?"

"Never mind."

He looked agitated and worried. It wasn't a put-on for my benefit. It was real and it made me even more confused and uneasy. But I wasn't about to let him know that.

"Everything fits, don't you see?" I said with confidence, "The wine bottle. The bad smell of wine in the room. The bloody clothes I saw near our garbage can. The clochard must have put on normal clothes so nobody would notice him going in the building, then after they got bloodied, changed back into his rags. When he was found he was wearing new shoes. And one more thing. He was very strong in spite of being a rummy. He pulled those heavy wagonloads through the streets. He could easily have picked up that bronze statue to kill Jacques and carried it away with him."

"Your theory is full of holes. That statue couldn't possibly have killed Jacques. And you said nothing about seeing the clochard when you were in the courtyard—and when would he have had time to change his clothes? The way you tell it, it all happened too quickly. Didn't the police come right after you went back to your apartment?"

"Not right after. And maybe the clochard didn't leave through the courtyard. Maybe he left through the rear window. You can step right out onto the roofs like in our bedroom. When I got there, the window was open and the curtain was moving. He could have gone out over the rooftops and then changed his clothes."

"Over the roof tops?" Boris thought for a minute. "Now you're telling me something. But then he couldn't have put the bloody clothes near the garbage bin. And anyway, the garbage is removed every day."

"Someone else could have put them there later."

"Who?"

"The man who murdered him?"

I still wasn't ready to tell Boris about the person I saw taking a shopping bag from under the clochard the night he was found dead. Could the contents have been those bloody clothes? Or was it something else, something even more important?

"So where is Veronique?" Boris said, "She must know something and I need answers or I'm a goner."

He looked awful when he said that and I felt sorry for him. But sorry wasn't enough to make me confide in him.

"If my theory is correct, with David, whoever he is."

"Your theory's rubbish."

We were walking past Les Halles, past the ancient carousel, past sleeping clochards, past the political satirists filling the air with typical Parisian enthusiasm.

"Boris, be straight with me, what's your part in all this?"

He stopped and turned to me, silent for a moment, then said, "I can't tell you just yet, but you have to trust me, you have to trust me enough to tell me everything you know." He looked grim. "If you can't maybe you should butt out. You're just getting in everybody's way."

"Who everybody?" I felt agitated. "Is this what you dragged me away from Sol to tell me? All I did was try to help Veronique. After that I was pulled into it. I didn't invite the police into my home. I didn't kidnap myself. I'd be happy to butt out if they let me—and when I know Veronique's okay. No one else seems to care. I have to go now. Sol's expecting me."

We started back. Boris was right. I didn't trust him. We didn't trust each other and both of us were holding out. The only way he could gain my confidence was to tell me about his involvement in this business. I guess he felt the same way.

"You are in over your head, Goldie. Come on, spit it out."

On impulse I asked, "Boris, are you King David?" He looked shocked.

"Jesus. I'm married to the sexiest woman in Paris. What do I need with Veronique? Besides, your theory is bullshit. How many times do I have to tell you?"

"Right. To change the subject. That creep who's been following me around, the one with the yellow shirt, do you know who he is?"

"Sure. A plainclothesman. He's protecting you."

"Call him off."

"Talk to the police. It has nothing to do with me."

"Why should I believe you? He looks like a criminal. And you told me yourself, you're involved with the underworld."

"I didn't say involved. I said acquainted. And this man is a policeman."

"He's a criminal. I should know. I had in my special Ed classes kids who grew up to be gangsters. I know the type. I can smell them. Get him off my back."

"When you get an idea in your head, Goldie…"

"You should have seen his face when I looked over his shoulder at his newspaper and saw the picture of Jacques lying dead."

"It's his job to watch people's reactions."

"I don't need watchers. I don't want to see that man again, do you hear, Boris, call him off."

"How can I? I'm not his boss. Goldie I'm your friend, not your enemy. You trusted me for thirty years. Did I ever do anything to betray that trust?"

We were waiting for a red light. "Not until now. But you haven't convinced me you're innocent. I'm not saying you actually had anything to do with the murder. I don't think you have it in you. And I suspect it was the clochard. But you didn't want me to talk to the police, and that makes me suspicious. For all I know, you had something to do with my abduction."

We were in the middle of the boulevard when he stopped and turned to me with an expression of outrage.

"You can't believe that Goldie!"

"Prove me wrong." The light changed and we dashed to the other side where we stopped and faced each other again.

His face softened. "Let me try to explain. I didn't want you to go to the police because I didn't want you to convince them that the statue is real. It's safer for me if they believe it's all in your imagination so I can find it before they do. But Goldie, you aren't accusing me of having something to do with your abduction?"

"It wasn't an accusation, it was more a question."

"I'm not in any way involved with Jacques' death. But I am involved with the statue you saw in Veronique's apartment. That's all I can tell you now."

Against my better judgment, I started to believe him. I felt suddenly ashamed of having doubted him. Maybe I'm a gullible dope but there seemed to be an aura of truth in what he said. Maybe if I gave a little he would also.

"Boris, do you think I should go to the police about being kidnapped?"

"You haven't told them?"

"It's a matter of communication. I can't go by myself. And that's not all I have to tell them."

We were standing near the darkened Russian gallery in my building. "What else?"

"I found out where they were hiding me and Veronique."

"Where?"

"Would you believe? There, right there in the basement under the gallery."

I could see a shudder go through him, then he composed himself.

"I'll go with you to the police station tomorrow morning, if you like."

"Thanks, Boris."

"Do you remember the name of the inspector?"

"Potiron, Hugues de Potiron."

"Ah—the pumpkin head."

"Please, Boris, don't let him talk to me in English. I couldn't take it."

CHAPTER THIRTEEN

Sol was in the library of the Pompidou Center the next morning doing research for his book. He didn't know I was on my way to the police station to meet Boris and Inspector Potiron. A few months ago I wouldn't have believed it was in me deceive him.

I followed rue Rambuteau past neighborhood shops, across the plaza, and onto a narrowed street with displays of fruits and vegetables and skirts of odorous garbage, until the street quieted down and became rue Francois Bourgeois with its raw sienna houses and the occasional boutique.

As I passed the National Archives and turned and walked and turned and walked again through the ancient streets of the Marais, I felt I was floating through a dream of centuries past, peopled by Moliere characters in sumptuous costumes. The images soothed my angst.

Too soon the solid reality of the police station loomed in front of me. I shook off the ancient images as the very contemporary Boris greeted me in front of a sand-colored old building. The cops standing around the entrance ignored us as we went in.

Ordinary people sat on benches unnoticed by busy police. Boris nodded at some of the officers and approached a desk. For someone trying to avoid the police he seemed right at home. After a few minutes of discussion we were given directions and sent on our way, up gray stone stairs and into a gloomy high ceilinged hallway. Boris stopped and knocked on a door.

"Entrez."

We walked in. There, sitting at a desk with his head bowed over some papers, his hair blanched by a wide shaft of sunlight, was Doctor Caligari, from the movie of the same name. After a moment, he lifted his face and smiled. For a fraction of a second, I thought I was in Caligari's madhouse and that the somnambulist in black tights would come floating through the door and lie down in a coffin.

But no, it was Inspector Potiron and he seemed to be acquainted with Boris. I didn't know if that was good or bad.

We sat down in front of the desk. Thank God we weren't touching noses this time.

"I hope the Madame, he goes well."

"He goes well," I said, looking meaningfully at Boris.

Boris took the cue. I heard him telling Inspector Potiron that he was there to translate, the inspector didn't need to bother speaking his excellent English. The young man with the notebook entered and stood at attention with poised pen.

"Tell him I was abducted. Tell him the whole story."

Boris complied, and ended by letting the Inspector know the location of the cellar, and suggesting, since they still had a man in the courtyard, it wouldn't hurt to have him investigate. But Boris omitted to mention that my captors were interested only in the statue of Bathsheba.

"They might find fingerprints and bits of stuff down there," I suggested.

"They know what they are doing, Goldie. They are professionals."

Inspector Potiron digested what Boris had said, shook his head, got up, and walked around his desk. As he advanced, I stood up and backed away. He followed me, put his face close to mine and touched the yellowing mouse under my eye with his fingertip.

"How are you having this?"

"Tell him how I got the mouse Boris, quickly, he had garlic for breakfast."

Boris told him.

Inspector Potiron looked skeptical as he went back to his desk.

The interview was over.

But something good came out of it. I was beginning to feel that Boris was on my side. Maybe it was that he was willing to expose himself, in spite of his fears, by coming to the police with me. A bud of trust had begun to sprout in the hard earth of doubt.

As we walked into the bright morning, Boris turned to me. "He doesn't believe anything, Goldie. He thinks you hurt your eye walking into a wall. That's what Americans do. I have to tell you his record for solving crimes isn't great."

"Why didn't you tell me that before we came?"

"I thought we might find out something from him."

"You are a conniving so and so!" But I forgave him.

"And did you find out anything?"

"Um. No."

Because I was beginning to trust him a little didn't mean I believed everything he said.

I couldn't understand most of what those two had been saying to each other, but Boris had come away with a strange look on his face. As we walked along the street he said to me, "Be careful, Goldie."

"I could say the same to you."

As we went our separate ways, I can't explain it, but I suddenly felt afraid for Boris.

CHAPTER FOURTEEN

After supper I felt edgy, like a puma in a cage stalking an invisible enemy.

"Sol, let's go for a walk, I feel a little nervous."

"I'm too tired. I haven't been getting much sleep lately."

"Then I'll go by myself, just for a couple of minutes. Don't worry. In this neighborhood there are plenty of cops on the street all hours."

"When did I ever stop you from going out by yourself in any kind of a neighborhood? Worrying is another story."

Tourists and cops and what have you were all over the place as I walked past the Pompidou Center. At St. Merri, the church that welcomes street people, I stopped for a moment of silence, to pay my respect to the clochard. An alto recorder whispered an elegy for the dead.

I was too antsy to stay for the rest of the concert. Instead, I walked back past the Stravinsky Fountain to the little square where people crowd together to listen to political diatribes. The atmosphere was like Union Square in the old days. I crossed Sebastopol to Pierre Lescot near the Forum Les Halles and went through the arcade to the carousel.

I watched as a few children rode the white horses with blue and green harlequin decorations, rising and falling, clinging to swirling gold poles above a bright red platform. Painted women, faded with time, looked down at them from the ceiling—Cleopatra, and Athena, and a lute player. The central trunk was encrusted with smudged mirrors surrounded by peeling gold curlicues. Suns and unicorns and stars, and two faded signs—"Manege Paul Loisel" and "Coppier, 17 rue St. monde, Montreuil Sous Bois," decorated the rest of it.

Points of light shimmied to canned accordion music. The scene made me homesick for when I used to take my kids to the carousel in Central park.

I walked back to rue Etienne Marcel, passing the tourist bistrots with people sitting at tables on the sidewalk. The hurdy-gurdy woman was arguing with one of the North Africans in front of the ancient brothel. I nodded to Madame Clara who was framed in her window, watching the kids playing below. Memories were awakened of the tenement streets of my childhood in New York where watchers kept the neighborhood safe for us. But this wasn't a New York Street, and I wasn't a child, and I didn't feel safe.

Before I turned into the arcade of my building, something caught my attention. The door to the box depository across the street was open and a light was on. It should have been locked up hours ago. I crossed over and looked in. I hadn't intended to enter, but no one was there so I took a few steps. I still didn't see anyone. I went further. If someone came I could always say I was looking for a box to mail a gift to America. America is a magic word to certain people in this country. They'll excuse anything if you tell them you're from the good old U.S.A.

Inside the large warehouse boxes were folded and stacked neatly in rows. A few bad paintings hung on a wall. I remembered that this place used to be an art gallery owned by a certain Arnaud Duvier. Maybe he abandoned them when he disappeared.

I was behind a row of boxes looking at the paintings on the wall when the light went out and I heard a door slam—and the sickening sound of a key in a lock.

"Hey," I cried out. But nobody heard, or chose not to. Oy, was I in a pickle! The last thing I wanted was to be locked up all night in a warehouse with a bunch of boxes. And what would the owner think—finding me there in the morning? And what would Sol think? Thoughts of all the deceit he was getting from me and all the pain I caused him during our long marriage shuddered through me. Never mind the past, what would he think when the truth about my current activities came to light? And it surely would—but not yet, I hoped.

I had to get out of that place. With the door closed, it began to smell like putrid fish. Who knows where those boxes had been? I felt my way to the door. I banged on it. I swallowed my dignity and shouted. No one came to my rescue. Of course not. There was enough noise in the street at that time of night to drown me out. And if someone did hear, they chose to ignore my cries. Besides, if nobody had come to the aid of Veronique when they saw her being strangled, why would they pay attention to shouts from a warehouse? I had to get out on my own. I felt around the door for a light switch, but I couldn't find one. I gave up and groped my way to the back. I was pretty nervous, I can tell you!

The back door was also locked. The window near it was painted closed and I couldn't budge it. I made an instant decision to break the window. What choice did I have? If Inspector Potiron found out, he would throw his sneering exotic English at me. So who cares?

Feeling my way in the dark, I groped for something heavy. I stumbled on an iron doorstop, picked it up, hesitated a minute, then heaved it through the window and jumped back. The glass shattered.

After pushing out most of the jagged pieces, and in the process cutting my hand, I climbed out into a narrow yard that backed on several buildings. I tried the doors. They were all locked. One of them looked like it belonged to the ancient hotel.

Then I saw the faces of children squashed against the ground floor window, watching me. They didn't respond to my gestures for help. I could see that the window was open a crack on the bottom, but it was too high to reach. I looked for something to stand on. Nothing. I gave up and walked back toward the warehouse thinking there might be a box inside—not looking forward to climbing back through the window.

Then I looked up and saw the all-night dress designer who lived in the building next to the ancient hotel. His window was open and he was peeing. I blushed and looked away. When the sound stopped I squelched my embarrassment and called up to him. When he looked down at me, I asked him to please open the door and let me in so I could go home.

He was down in a minute. We introduced ourselves. I was relieved that he could speak English. He said his name was Dimitri Lenotre. He recognized me from seeing me through his window. Odd, I'd never seen him lift his face from his work to glance outside. On the night of the riot in the street, he was engrossed in his work, not in the "Theater of the Absurd," like the rest of us.

I told him what happened. He was sympathetic, not judgmental. Up close, I could see he had blond hair pulled back in a ponytail. His eyes were a pale cerulean blue. When I held out my hand to shake his, it was dripping blood. I wondered what he could be thinking of me—a stranger with a bloody hand appearing in his back yard.

He put a clean silk handkerchief around my hand and led me inside, up a white marble staircase into an entry with a black white and tile floor dotted with drops of my blood.

"If you give me a rag I'll clean it up fast."

"It's not a problem.

The bathroom was a fantasy, his, not mine-pink with small marble angels embracing soap dishes, and gold angels holding up an old-fashioned bathtub. Dimitri took cotton, alcohol and a tweezers out of a medicine cabinet, and like a gentle nurse, removed the slivers of glass I didn't know were there, then cleaned the cuts in my hands. They were small—only needing band-aids. I hoped Sol wouldn't notice. As he put his supplies away, I saw Dimitri's face in the light. It was delicate, like a Memling portrait.

"Would you like to see my studio?" he asked.

"Of course." What I could see from my window intrigued me and I wasn't disappointed. There were dressmaker's dummies with all kinds of exotic clothes and bits and pieces of fabric and feathers and spangles everywhere. Dominating the room was an enlarged photo of a woman with sleek black hair cut in a pageboy from out of the twenties. I did a double take. It was Veronique! I guess Dimitri noticed.

"Yes, it's Veronique. Taken by Man Ray a few years ago."

"You're a friend of Veronique?"

"We are acquainted," he said.

"I wish I knew where she was. She disappeared, you know."

"Did she?" He didn't sound concerned.

"You don't know? It was in all the papers," I said.

"I don't have time to read newspapers."

"I guess not. No matter how late I'm up, I always see you working."

"I've been getting ready for my show tomorrow night."

"Then I better leave," I told him.

"I'm finished now. I allow myself a day to relax."

"I've never been to a fashion show."

"I'm not an important designer. I've never been affiliated with a major house and I can't compete with the brilliant newcomers."

"I don't know anything about fashion, as you can see by how I dress, but I bet you're as good as anyone."

He responded with a shrug. He didn't look bitter, and he couldn't be doing too badly as I could see by his house. At least he had a shot at it. Maybe he hadn't made it big, but at least he was designing clothes. Me? My only career in art was painting eyes on ducks in a toy factory when I graduated from art school.

"My show is in a loft in the eleventh arrondisement. It won't be anything special."

"It would be special to me," I told him.

I saw him hesitate before he offered me an invitation.

"Don't expect too much," he said.

"Thanks. I wouldn't know how to judge."

"Take someone with you. It's not a neighborhood for a woman to be in alone at night."

CHAPTER FIFTEEN

I was wrong. Sol did notice the band-aids on my hand and he didn't buy my lies, I could tell by the hurt look in his eyes. But he said nothing. Silence was the only way he could cope with my peculiar behavior.

The next morning he left for the library without his usual croissant. I felt bad, but his absence gave me the opportunity for a quiet think.

The only person who knew about my Bathsheba theory was Boris and he thought it was rubbish. I needed more information to support it. Where to start? Sylvie seemed to have a nose for rumors. It was time for a private chat with the demon of nighttime television.

I could hear her TV even though it was daytime. Maybe she had taken the day off to make up for the all-night recording session. I decided to invite myself up for morning coffee and try to pump her for information. She took the bait and asked me in. It was a chance for her to do her favorite thing after TV, complain about men and life. As she was making the coffee in the kitchen, I clicked my camera on her furniture, which was tacky modern, and her paintings which were contemporary crap. I looked out of the back window and saw the perpetual cop in front of Batiment B. in my courtyard. I could also see Veronique's window.

Sylvie came back with the coffee and a bottle of brandy. She filled her cup with a lot of brandy and a drop of coffee. She filled mine with unadulterated coffee, which is the way I like it. I sat on the edge of her sofa.

"I was looking at your art collection."

"It's hardly art. I got those paintings from the Arnaud Duvier gallery that used to be across the street. It was considered chic to buy from him, and the pictures were cheap, like he was."

"You knew him?"

"Didn't I? Why not? Everyone did. He wasn't a shrinking violet. When he disappeared there were people who thought something terrible happened to him. But I didn't. Arnaud was a victimizer, not a victim. Arnaud is indestructible."

All that brandy was making her talkative. Good. "You haven't seen him since?"

"Not true. I saw him a few days ago on the street, not that he acknowledged my existence."

"Where was he all those years?"

"Who knows? Who cares."

"Do you think he'll open another gallery?"

"Why? He knows nothing about art. The gallery was a front. He's a criminal and a police informer. When he gets caught he knows the police will go easy on him."

"Did Arnaud know Veronique." I knew the answer, but I wanted to hear what she had to say.

"Are you kidding? They had a love nest in her apartment which her previous lover had bought for her." She nodded at the back window. "Their lover's quarrels were grand opera on the street."

"Why did they break up?"

"She had another lover on the sly. No one knows who it was. Arnaud only found out about it when she became pregnant."

"Maybe it was his?"

"No way. He couldn't have kids. Low sperm count or something. Everyone knew about that too. Maybe that was why he acted so macho. He gave her such a beating when he found out, that she ended up in the hospital. It's a miracle she and her unborn child survived, not that I care. It's only a matter of time for her."

"What does that mean?"

"Nothing."

"Did the child survive?"

"Sure. The kid's living with a relative outside Paris. I'm sick of all this." She made a grand gesture. "When my boat comes in, which should be any day now, I'll be out of here like a shot. I'm going to live in a big house in the country like your proprietaire."

"Do you think he's mixed up in Jacques' murder?"

"Your guess is as good as mine. Why not? Anybody could be. You could be."

"Are you?" I knew I shouldn't have said it, but I couldn't help myself.

Her eyes scrunched into slits. "You didn't come here for a sociable cup of coffee, did you? You came here to grill me. I'm tired. I have a headache, Madame."

Madame? Just a few minutes ago I was Goldie to her.

Before I left I entered into my files mental pictures of her face and body from all angles. There was something odd and stiff about the way she moved as she showed me to the door.

At home, I put her out of my mind as I puttered through my clothes to find something decent to wear for Dimitri's show that night. I didn't want to shame him, but I didn't have anything elegant. So who was going to look at me, especially at a fashion show?

Sol refused to come. He had no interest in schmattas, he told me. Also he was mad at me for staying out so long on my walk the night before. Thank God he didn't know what really happened. I had explained the Band-Aids with a cock-and-bull story about tripping on the street. I told him Dimitri helped me up and happened to have Band-Aids in his pocket.

Maxi was more than willing to go with me. She was particular about what she put on that slim body of hers and was hoping she'd find a dress she liked. I suspected she thought she'd get it wholesale since I was a friend of the designer. Friend? Not yet. I had only made his acquaintance the day before. My motivation for going was the hope that it would lead me to King David, a man with an eye for the girls. It didn't lead me to King David, it led me to tragedy.

CHAPTER SIXTEEN

Maxi parked near the Bastille. As we walked away from the cozy, lit up restaurants and lively crowds, we entered a maze of darkened side streets with shabby tenements, warehouses, and the occasional gentrified dwelling with geraniums spilling over sills. In Paris, affluence often lives side by side with poverty. Though I wish everyone was rich, I enjoy the camaraderie and intermingling.

The streets were empty of people but filled with a kind of heavy stillness. I was a little uneasy in spite of the street smarts I had imported from New York. Maxi was Maxi, unflappable. She thinks Paris is the safest city in the world.

She was thoughtful during our solitary tramp, giving one word responses to my lame efforts at conversation so I gave up. It was taking a long time to get there and I wondered if Maxi knew where she was going. If she didn't, she wouldn't admit it, but after a while I became aware of the odd sound, the occasional footstep.

Suddenly straggles of people appeared around us, talking and laughing, and the stillness evaporated. We got in step with a bunch of expensive looking oddballs. I assumed they were going to Dimitri's fashion show and it turned out I was right. I have to admit, I was glad for the company.

Would you believe, my Goddamned shadow was with them-escorting a befurred woman-in August yet? If he was a plainclothesman protecting me, as Boris had said, where was he when I was locked in that warehouse? Oh well. Best thing was to ignore him.

When we arrived at the loft, it was already filled with people. Leave it to Maxi to always be late. People in fancy schmattas were sitting on folding chairs or standing around at the back talking. We found seats reserved for us in front, near the ramp that cut the room in half.

It was an informal sort of affair. Skinny models wearing outlandish clothes and feathers and sequins and I don't know what else, were standing around in various postures on the platform, while Dimitri made a speech I couldn't understand. He got laughs, which surprised me—he didn't seem the humorous type. Maxi was enchanted by him. Too bad for her he was gay, at least I thought he was.

After the speech, the models formed a pattern on the stage, then slithered, one by one, down the ramp draped in Dimitri's whimsical creations. As clothes for the average working person, they were too theatrical, but as theater they were great. All the models wore that Patsy-doll hairstyle from the twenties and thirties—the kind I saw on that blow-up of Veronique on Dimitri's wall.

One of them was more weird then the others. She wore a veil over her face and each time she came down the ramp she seemed more familiar until...

"Veronique!" I shouted, before I could stop myself. I couldn't stop myself from running after her up the ramp like an idiot, almost knocking down the other models waiting on the platform. I dashed into the dressing room where young women in various states of undress stared at me in alarm. I searched for Veronique among them, but couldn't find her.

As I looked for a door the situation brought back a flash of memory: I was young, I had a job taking market surveys in New York when I walked unknowingly into a brothel in Hell's Kitchen. It was an amazingly similar scene of young women sitting around half-naked—but this wasn't a brothel in Hell's kitchen. It was a dressing room at a fashion show in Paris—and Veronique had disappeared again. Dimitri materialized, looking more sad then angry. I didn't give him a chance to say anything. I apologized and ran back down the ramp to Maxi.

"We have to go now," I told her, crouching in the aisle, trying not to block the view.

"If you want to go, go. I'm staying."

"But you shouldn't walk alone in these streets, Maxi."

"Don't be silly. I have my car."

"But it's a long way to your car."

"I can take care of myself, Goldie."

That was true. I was wasting my time arguing with her. I ran outside.

To my surprise, Veronique was waiting for me in the shadows. Under the heavy make-up I could see that her face was swollen and covered with bruises.

"I'm so glad I found you," was all I could think of to say.

"Let's take a walk."

We strolled in silence, arm-in-arm, among warehouses and empty tenements. I was savoring my relief in finding her. We entered another neighborhood, streets of charming old buildings and darkened boutiques. Old Paris sometimes opens up like that, like a flower blossoming in the sun. But there was no sun. It was night.

When she finally spoke, in a mixture of English and French, her words were drowned in my overwhelming emotions at finding her. I stopped and touched her face.

"Did those goons in the cellar do that to you?"

"Just Arnaud."

I already knew something about Arnaud and now I realized he was one of the two men in the cellar. "Why?"

"Why not? Beating women is a habit some men never grow out of."

"When you lived together?" She nodded. "How could you let him?"

"It's hard to explain. He was so handsome and strong, and he could be so tender and vulnerable when he wasn't raging with jealousy. He could make me feel it was the me inside he loved, not my looks. That sounds like a cliché but for me its true. Being beautiful is an affliction. I sometimes wanted to ruin my face, now Arnaud has done it for me."

"Poor Veronique."

"Don't feel sorry for me. I brought it on myself."

"Nonsense! That's what abused women always say and it isn't true."

We had arrived at the place where the St. Martin canal starts its underground journey toward the Bastille. We stopped a minute to admire the footbridges that rose in pale green iron arcs over the water, one after the other into the distance. I had a strong desire to paint this scene. But it was not for me. It was for a great painter like Monet.

We took the cobblestone path along one side of the canal. There were no barriers to keep people from stepping into the inky depths if they chose. I gently eased Veronique away from the edge.

"How did you escape from the cellar?" I asked her.

"After they dragged you away and came back, Arnaud and the Russian decided it wasn't wise to keep me there. They were sure you'd figure out where you had been and tell the police."

"They thought I was smarter than I was," I told her. "Go on."

"They dragged me up the stairs and out into the street. As they were shoving me into their car, I got away from them and ran down to the cafe. I was too fast for them. They drove away without me. My good angel Dimitri saw what was happening in the street, and came for me, and hid me in his house."

So Dimitri had lied to me. She had been in his house all this time—even when I was there. Oh well, maybe he had a good reason.

"Veronique, did you see who killed Jacques?"

"No. I have no idea who did it."

Was she lying too?

"But I saw Jacques trying to strangle you and when I got to your apartment, he was dead and you were gone."

"I didn't know he was dead until Dimitri told me."

"Why was Jacques trying to strangle you?"

"For a silly reason."

"What was that?"

We were walking past the locks with iron gates that opened for the boats that carried tourists. Perhaps the canal was still used for commerce. I didn't know. The gates were closed now. On the other side of the canal was a small brick building with the words "Ecluses de Temple" on it, mirrored on the smooth face of the water.

"I was upset because Jacques brought home that horrible statue. He said it was extremely valuable. He said he had put himself in great danger to get it. He said he would be paid a lot of money for it. We had to keep it until Arnaud came for it.

"I thought he was lying. Arnaud had disappeared years ago. And I couldn't stand having that statue among my beautiful things. I wanted that awful piece of junk out of my apartment. Jacques refused. I told him to leave it outside the door. He laughed at me. So I became angry and got a kitchen knife and started slashing at it. That enraged him. When I wouldn't stop, he tried to kill me. Over that piece of garbage, that papier Mache statue!"

"Papier mache?" I was surprised. "So the statue wasn't bronze? Then it couldn't have been the murder weapon."

"I don't think so."

"But it was covered in blood when I saw it."

"I don't know about that," she said.

"So what was the murder weapon?" I wondered.

"I don't know. Maybe the kitchen knife?"

That was a thought.

"How did you get away from Jacques?"

"It was because of you. When you shouted at him, he let go of me and shut the window. I ran out. Near your building, I heard someone coming down the stairs, but I didn't know who it was so I went out the gate. The gallery was all lit up and the door was open. There were two men in there—and one of them was Arnaud! So Jacques was telling the truth! I was shocked to see him after all those years. I stopped. Before I knew it, the gallery light was turned out and Arnaud grabbed me and pulled me inside and dragged me down into the cellar."

"So that's why you said "Arnaud" to me in the cellar?"

"Yes. I don't know who the other man was but he had a Russian accent. I told Arnaud that I ran out because Jacques was trying to strangle me because of some stupid statue."

Was Arnaud King David? I wondered.

"Veronique, do you think Arnaud killed Jacques—to get you back?"

"Not at all. We were finished years ago, when he disappeared. Besides, he couldn't have killed Jacques. He was in the cellar with me. He only wanted to know about that stupid papier mache statue. Why is everyone is so interested in it?"

A good question. I also wanted to know. So Arnaud wasn't King David. So who was? My Bathsheba theory was beginning to disintegrate as the bronze turned to papier mache.

Veronique continued, "I told Arnaud the statue was in my apartment and Jacques was expecting him. I would be happy if he would take it away. I hated it. He ran up the cellar stairs. He only got as far as the gallery when heard someone in the courtyard and came back down."

"It must have been the clochard."

"What?"

"Nothing. Go on."

"Arnaud was furious. He said that if I hadn't come by when I did, he would have the statue by now."

"He couldn't have. It was gone by then," I told her.

"He didn't know that. By the time he was finished yelling, we heard sirens. That made him even more furious, and he beat me with his fists until the Russian stopped him. Then he went upstairs to see what was happening. When he came down, he said there was so much confusion they could sneak out without being noticed, but they couldn't risk taking me with them.

"I begged them not to leave me behind I was terrified of being alone with the rats. I had been bitten when I was a child. But Arnaud shoved me back down the steps. I said the gallery owner would come and find me. Arnaud said the gallery had gone out of business. No one was interested in crappy Russian art. He locked the cellar door."

"Those schmucks!" I said.

We had come to a car bridge over the St. Martin canal. I could see the curved ruts where the road turned aside to open the canal so the boats could go through. Veronique stopped and turned to me.

"Goldie, why did Arnaud bring you to the cellar?"

"I can only guess that he believed I knew where the statue was. Since Arnaud is a police informer—maybe it works both ways. I told the police I had seen the statue, and they probably passed the information on to him. The statue was the only thing the Russian asked me about when I was in the cellar."

"Do you know where it is?"

"I haven't the foggiest idea. It was still in your apartment when I left. In the beginning the police believed you murdered Jacques."

"Me?"

"I know it's stupid. A lot of people saw you being strangled—but did nothing about it. Now those same people have decided to become good citizens and tell the police what they saw." We started back along the path.

"It doesn't matter. Tomorrow Dimitri is taking me and my son to the south of France to stay with my aunt."

"Oh, good." I felt momentary relief.

We were back where the canal fled under the tunnel. From there I could see the lights and the huge statue in the Place de la Republic a block away. I knew the metro was waiting there to take me to rue Rambuteau and home to Sol.

"I have to go back to Dimitri now," Veronique said.

"No, don't. Come home with me."

"I can't, I have to go back now."

"Then I'll go with you. I won't let you go alone."

She was suddenly running away from me and I couldn't possibly catch up with her at my age. Oh well, by this time tomorrow she'd be far away and out of danger.

But I was wrong.

The next morning Veronique was found floating in the canal, her body pressed against the iron gate of the lock near the small brick building with "Ecluse du Temple" over the door. The article in the newspaper described a blue crucifix tattooed on her arm.

CHAPTER SEVENTEEN

Anger over Veronique's death dulled my grief. Whoever had murdered her so brutally would answer to me. I guess that sounds pompous. Who was I to make such a statement? A retired special Ed teacher doesn't have the tools to solve crimes, but I was determined to try, even if I infuriated Inspector Potiron and ended in prison with all those French criminals and prostitutes and drug dealers.

I was the last person to see Veronique alive, except for the murderer. Why else would inspector Potiron want to see me again?

Sol knew almost everything now, it was in the newspapers, including my being thrown into that cellar with Veronique, which made him crazy. He couldn't stand to think that his beloved me had been damaged. He didn't care so much that I had lied to him.

He wouldn't have known about the cellar if I hadn't gone to the police and told them. Too bad Inspector Potiron decided to believe me and blabbed to the newspapers. At least Sol didn't know about my being locked in the box depository. Anyway, that didn't turn out so badly. I got to know Dimitri because of that misadventure.

Sol said if I hadn't met Dimitri and gone to the fashion show, I wouldn't have been the last person to see Veronique alive, and the police wouldn't be on my back now. I was poking my nose where it didn't belong, as usual.

It suddenly hit me that if I hadn't gone to that show, Veronique would not have run out and maybe she would still be alive. Oh God! But then again maybe she would have been murdered no matter what I did. That's what Sylvie had implied the last time I saw her. No, it was my fault. Better not to think about it or I would melt away in guilt trauma.

With all that was going on in my head I had no time to mourn Veronique. But maybe that was a good thing. For me mourning is like a deep depression that keeps me from functioning. And I needed to function. I needed to find answers.

Sol was more vehement about going home to New York now. But we couldn't—I was definitely in the witness category, and I might even be a suspect. Me! Goldie Yampolski, nee Goldberg of Jackson Heights. I was notorious. I wouldn't get past customs at Roissy. I couldn't go home, and I didn't want to. I wanted to find Veronique's murderer. I wanted to see him punished.

I was a celebrity on our block. All the crumbling old buildings had eyes that were judging me as I walked down the street. But my human neighbors averted their eyes and Sylvie cut me dead, you should excuse the expression.

The only person who looked at me was my shadow with the upside-down pear face, always there, always watching. My protector? I never believed that. If someone decided to kill me, would he try to save me? Not on your life. He would watch my last gasp and report it to whomever he was reporting to. And I didn't believe his boss was Inspector Potiron. Boris was wrong about him, or maybe he had lied. Everybody was lying, Dimitri, Sylvie—even me.

Maxi wasn't talking to me. She was mad at me for uncovering blemishes on the tush of her beloved France. She wasn't talking to me in spite of the fact that if it hadn't been for me she wouldn't have that designer dress to wear at the fancy champagne opening of her exhibition of paintings.

Dimitri gave her the dress. This is how it happened. When Veronique ran out on him during the fashion show, he asked Maxi to model

Veronique's other dresses. She's the same size-can you imagine? Maxi was happy to oblige. As a result she had the pick of his schmattas.

Ginger peachy for Maxi. As for me, I was trying to keep my head above a pool of guilt. As a result of my stupidity Veronique was dead. My Bathsheba theory was rubbish—Bathsheba was just a name given to that crummy papier mache statue for no reason. David had not walked out of the tapestries at Ecouen to become Dimitri, or Arnaud, or Boris. David, if he existed, would never kill the woman he loved. Oh well it wouldn't be the last time I was wrong.

The night after they found Veronique's body, I saw Dimitri through the window at his work table. His head was down and his back was heaving with sobs. His pain made mine seem insignificant.

The next morning our bell rang. It was Dimitri. He asked, through the intercom, if I could stay with Veronique's son Pascal while he went to Gare Montparnasse to get tickets to take him to Veronique's aunt in the South. With all the scandal in the newspapers, the relative caring for the boy outside Paris no longer wanted to be responsible.

"Wait, I'll put my shoes on. I'm coming right down."

"Goldie, where are you going?"

"To Dimitri's, to baby-sit Veronique's son."

"I haven't even met the guy. What are you getting yourself into now? Can't you stay out of other people's business for a change?"

"It's okay. I'm just babysitting. It's the least I can do."

"Goldie…What goes on here when I'm at the library?"

"I can't talk. He's waiting for me." I blew Sol a kiss. He wiped it off his cheek.

Dimitri ushered me into a small library. Books covered the walls. An oak desk in the middle of the room was surrounded by black leather arm chairs and low tables.

The boy was about six. A doll. He looked just like his mother, with jet black hair, but blue eyes instead of brown. He was sitting like an angel in one of the stuffed armchairs with a book in his hand. He looked up when we walked in.

"Pascal, C'est Madame Goldie." I was glad he didn't say Madame Yampolski. That would have been a mouthful for a little French boy.

Pascal stood up and kissed me on each cheek, with little birdlike pecks. "Bonjour, Madame."

So polite. Not like the hooligans I teach. Mind you, not all of my charges were bad—some of them grew up to be decent citizens, and some even became rich and famous. But this boy was a bookworm. It would be an easy baby-sit.

"I won't be long," said Dimitri.

"Take your time, we'll be fine. I don't suppose Pascal speaks English."

"He doesn't, but you can teach him."

As soon as Dimitri was gone, Pascal put a Babar bookmark in his book and placed it carefully on the table. He made a sign for me to follow him through a door that led out of the library and into a hall. The walls were hung with fine etchings and delicate water colors. From there a door opened into a large room. The first things I noticed were the sketches and paintings of Veronique all over the walls. It was as though Dimitri was obsessed with her.

"Maman," Pascal said.

"I know. Je sais." With an ache in my chest, I wondered if the boy knew that his mother was dead. I couldn't believe anyone would have the heart to tell him.

He took my hand and we went into the hall again. He led me up a flight of stairs and into a bedroom filled with antiques. A heavy wooden canopied four-poster bed decorated in red velvet dominated the room. Beautiful little still lifes were hung on the walls. My camera clicked, even without my directing it.

Pascal took my hand again and we walked into a smaller bedroom, very simple, with a low bed and a few stuffed animals. He picked up a lamb and I followed him out and down the stairs to the library. He sat down on the stuffed chair, picked up his book and was soon lost in it.

I looked at the soft curve of his cheek. A Modigliani face. If I were to pick up my brushes again I would paint him. I wondered what he was reading, what he was thinking, what sort of life he had led during his short time on earth. He looked up at me from his book. I was embarrassed and turned my eyes away. I poked around the bookshelves. Everything was in French, but there were quite a few art books. I looked at a Matisse book, and another on Russian icons. But I couldn't keep my mind on them because I kept seeing Veronique's face on all the pages.

I sat down and tried to relax. It was difficult. The events of the past few days were clouding my thoughts, and now that my Bathsheba theory was washed up I couldn't make much sense of anything.

I only knew that the two murders had something to do with the papier mache statue of Bathsheba. But what? Since the statue was junk, could some sort of treasure have been hidden in it? Treasure valuable enough for someone to commit murder over it? Could Arnaud and Jacques have been working together—Jacques stealing the statue, and Arnaud disposing of the contents? That was pretty much what Veronique told me when we spoke near the canal.

If that was the plan, it wasn't carried out, because someone else got to the statue first. I still believed that someone else was the clochard and he had killed Jacques to get it. But what was hidden inside the statue and who hired him to steal it? Did the shopping bag I saw taken from under the clochard when he was lying dead in the street contain the treasure everyone was looking for?

I was sure I was the only one who had seen that episode. I shared that secret with no one, not the police, not Boris. Why not? I couldn't even explain it to myself.

I concentrated on trying to identify the person who had taken the shopping bag. I called up pictures of the scene from my mental files and saw a figure bending over the clochard and taking the shopping bag.

The hat was pulled down and what I saw of the face was blurred. I looked at the pictures over and over again, at the movements of the body, until it gradually dawned on me that they were not masculine gestures. That person moved like a woman—or a man with the gestures of a woman. I couldn't be sure which. The angle of the body was very distinctive and slightly familiar. Who was it? The shadow at the edge of my mind never came into focus.

I thought of the fight in the street that night. Had it been staged to divert attention from the clochard so that the treasure could be removed?

My thoughts were interrupted by Dimitri's return. I was so deep in my own world, I was barely aware of his expressions of gratitude as I left, but I know I got two pecks from Pascal.

When I arrived home, Sol informed me that Inspector Potiron wanted to see me in my own "milieu."

CHAPTER EIGHTEEN

Inspector Potiron wanted to interview me in my own milieu? Was he making a study of the peculiar workings of the American mind? I wondered. Boris had kindly interrupted work on his newest invention just to translate for me. Or did he have an ulterior motive?

This time I positioned the dining table between us, a master stroke, since Inspector Potiron was still aromatic from his lunch. Sol cleared off his papers. Even if he had owned a beautiful big desk he would still spread his work all over dining table. I had long ago given up on a tidy living room.

That day he didn't go to the library. He watched the circus from his perch half-way up the stairs to the balcony. Boris sat next to me, the man with the notebook sat next to the inspector.

"Why you tell me not statue papier mache?"

Statue? Did Potiron finally believe in the statue?

"Oh really, Boris. If you came to translate for me do it!"

"Calm down. I think you get the gist of the question."

"Okay, tell him I had no idea the statue was papier mache. It looked like bronze to me. I learned it was papier mache from Veronique before she was killed."

Boris and Inspector Potiron had a heated discussion and from then on Boris translated for both of us.

I was grilled for more than an hour. Potiron surprised me. He wanted to know every little detail of the fashion show. Of course I had to tell him that Maxi was there. He looked severely at Boris and there was another discussion.

Boris said, "He insists Maxi should be with us now. He has questions to ask her. I told him he didn't invite her. He wants me to call her and tell her to come now. I told him that was impossible. I don't know where she is."

"God, Boris, I'm sorry I involved her. She has no time for this. She has to get ready for her exhibition."

"It's not your fault. You have to answer his questions."

Inspector Potiron turned to me and said, "This is not time for head to head. Every people is important. Madame, when you are with Veronique on top of the canal are you see a people?"

"Well. I suppose so. We passed a few people. I didn't pay attention. I didn't know she was going to be murdered."

More French talk.

"He says you are not cooperating."

I glanced at Sol. He looked like he was about to squash that little man. I suppose he could have, but he didn't. Inspector Potiron wanted to know every word Veronique and I spoke to each other. He asked who the Russian in the cellar was. I said I didn't know, and I didn't.

I purposely didn't tell the inspector that Veronique had been staying with Dimitri. Why should I? All he knew was that she was his model and that's all he was going to know as far as I was concerned.

I endured Potiron's pointless questions until he was satisfied he could get no more out of me. Then he stood up. His sidekick closed the notebook. They shook hands with us and left.

I seldom drank alcohol out of frustration or stress, and certainly not in the middle of the day. But I invited Sol and Boris to a meal in a swanky restaurant of Boris' choosing. I would have a kir before lunch, and red Bordeaux during. The hell with it. Boris was happy to come since Maxi was too busy to cook her usual gourmet lunches. Sol tagged along, looking depressed.

CHAPTER NINETEEN

The telephone woke me up about eleven a.m. I couldn't believe I slept so late. I was just staggering out of bed when Sol handed me the phone. It was Maxie. She was furious with me for involving her with the police. Somehow Potiron had tracked her down and called her to the prefecture that morning. Not that she spent much time there. Inspector Potiron had already fallen head over heels in love with her in my apartment, in spite of the fact that she's American. But she had been interrupted in the middle of an important meeting with the gallery owner—and it was downright embarrassing.

Maxi had been giving me the silent treatment. But she broke her silence long enough to wake me up and yell at me and invite us to the opening of her exhibition that evening. A bit late, I'd say. But I accepted.

In addition, she was concerned about Boris. He was beginning to look haggard. I suggested, in jest, that it might be because she had been neglecting to cook her usual splendid meals for him as the opening, the vernissage, approached.

"Then he should learn to cook for himself," was her response as she hung up.

The show was on one of those gorgeous, typically Parisian streets in the sixth arrondisment, with muted facades opening to surprising courtyards awash with greenery. When we arrived, people were spilling out into the street drinking champagne out of stemmed plastic glasses and sucking olive pits. Vernissages are the only occasions I know of when French people arrive early. Maybe they want to make sure of a plentiful supply of booze.

It was some affair! I'm sure well-known artists were milling around but I wouldn't know who they were. I had lost track of art fads and current gallery sweethearts after I left art school. I was too busy surviving.

Champagne and fancy wine and salty nibbles were spread out on tables hidden behind crowds of imbibers. Other art lovers were standing in clumps like grapes on a vine, gossiping. Nobody but me seemed to be looking at the paintings. They were great. Sort of semi-abstract fish of various species swimming on the walls. From the hand of a less imaginative and skilled painter they might have been kitschy, but Maxi's fish had just the right touch of humor.

After I looked at all the paintings, I squeezed between walls of people to get at the food. I avoided the bowls of nuts and crackers and olives. I'm still squeamish about dipping my hands in food where so many others have been. I didn't abstain from the little frankfurters wrapped in flaky dough, which I could spear with a toothpick, called pigs-in-blankets in the States. I devoured little squares of bread with cucumbers and shrimp. I hoped Sol was also eating, so I wouldn't have to make dinner that night.

As I escaped from the food I saw Maxi. Dimitri's creation looked sensational on her. Or she looked sensational it. Whatever. Of course, it wasn't as extreme as some of his other designs. Anyway, Maxi is the only person I know who can get away with wearing such a garment at her age. The reason, I suppose, is that she's so skinny and her neck is still smooth. Though I must say she has more facial wrinkles than I do. But with a little make-up, nobody notices.

She still has the dress, though she has never to my knowledge worn it since. It is a clingy, black, silky affair with a blue rose over the belly button. One shoulder and part of the back is missing and an electric-blue piece of schmatta covers her tush. This description is the best I can do.

Everybody but me was dressed to the gills. My second best Lord and Tayler outfit was lying wherever the sanitation department had dumped it, and I was afraid for my first best dress, with all the people eating messy canapés and shoving each other. So I wore my usual. So what? Everyone doesn't have to be a clothes horse.

Maxi didn't have much time for me. Artists never do at openings. She was flitting from person to person like a black and blue butterfly. Boris didn't have much time for me either. While Maxi was hoping for potential buyers for her paintings, he was hoping to do deals with those who looked rich. It seemed to me a conflict of interest. Oh well. Sol was shyly conversing with a pretty young woman and blushing, so I decided to let him enjoy himself.

I interrupted Boris who was talking to another attractive woman. "I've been meaning to ask you who that man was I saw coming out of the Russian gallery with you a few days ago."

Boris turned a color I will not describe. Maybe it was the gallery lights.

"Shut up, Goldie," he whispered as he excused himself and steered me through the crowd and into the office at the back of the gallery.

"Goldie, don't you have any sense?" he said as he closed the door.

"Usually. What did I say?"

"If you don't know, there's no use in explaining."

What a pill! I decided to tell him about an idea I had been mulling over.

"You won't tell me who that man was? Okay. I'll tell you my new theory about what happened to the statue that disappeared from the murder scene that everyone is so interested in."

"Your theories are crap."

"What's the matter? Why are you talking to me like that?"

"Sorry, Goldie, I'm not in great shape."

"You could have fooled me."

"What's your theory?"

"I think that papier mache statue of Bathsheba was used to transport something really valuable. It's what was hidden in it, not the statue that everyone is interested in finding, including you, Boris. Am I right?"

"You're right and you're wrong. The statue itself is also of crucial importance to me. Tell me where it is, then you'll be telling me something."

"I can only tell you where I think it is. I think it's on a rooftop. I think it was thrown out the back window of Veroniques' living room by who-ever killed Jacques, probably the clochard. I believe the clochard removed whatever was in the statue and gave it to whoever hired him—and was killed for his trouble." I didn't tell Boris the whole story—that I had seen someone take a shopping bag from under the sleeping-or dead-clochard.

Boris seemed to be digesting what I said.

I added foolishly, "If someone were to climb out of the window and look for it, he might find the statue hidden among the roofs of Paris."

"How could that be done? The apartment is sealed off by the police. Haven't you noticed?"

"Yes I have. But you have pull with the government, don't you?"

"Not to get in there I don't"

"I told you before. The roofs just outside our bedroom window con-nect with Veronique's building."

Boris was quiet for a minute. He started to say something, then changed his mind.

"What?"

"Nothing. You'll be pleased to know that the police agree with you that it was the clochard who killed Jacques."

"Good for them! They finally got some sense. What convinced them?"

"His fingerprints are all over the place, especially outside the back window. What do you think caused the clochard's death, Goldie?"

"I think the person who hired him gave him a bottle of wine as par-tial payment for delivering the treasure to whoever. I think he got a bonus in a bottle of wine—poison."

"You got it on the nose. The coroner found poison in the autopsy and in the bottle of wine he was holding."

"He must have been hiding somewhere on the roofs outside the window while I was in the apartment. He must have come back after I left and taken what was in the statue then thrown it out the window. That's why the statue was missing from the picture in the newspaper.

"It all fits in with what Veronique told me. That night, after she was dragged into the cellar, Arnaud started to go to Veronique's apartment to get the statue, but had to turn back because he heard footsteps in the courtyard. He waited in the cellar until he thought it was safe to go up. But he waited too long because the police came really fast. He didn't know that the clochard had already taken whatever was in the statue. Boris, do you know what that was?"

"No, I don't. Listen, Goldie."

"What?"

"Does Sol ever take sleeping pills?"

"Never. Why are you asking such a question?"

"I need to get into your bedroom tonight without him knowing."

"Oh thrill. I didn't think you cared."

"I don't mean for that."

"I didn't think you did, Boris. You want to climb onto the roof and try to find the statue, right?"

"Right."

"It's ridiculous and dangerous."

"You gave me the idea."

"For a professional, not a bumbler like you."

"I don't trust anyone else and I have to find the statue. What do you say, Goldie?"

"I don't know why I should go along with you, but okay, since you seem to think it's so earth-shaking. Sol will be dead to the world by then. Nothing will wake him up."

"I'll be there around twelve. Listen, Goldie, this is a matter of life and death for me, don't screw things up."

"Okay, okay." The small room and his aura of fear were making me claustrophobic. "I hope there are some little frankfurters left," I said as I walked out of the office.

"Thanks Goldie. Say goodbye to Sol for me."

CHAPTER TWENTY

Lying awake in bed next to the somnolent Sol, I was getting very nervous. I deeply regretted telling Boris my theory about the statue. I was terrified at the thought that he would soon be climbing on the roofs outside. If he fell and got hurt or killed I'd have it on my conscience for the rest of my life. And what about poor Maxi? I was already imagining her fashionably dressed for the funeral.

He arrived at twelve as he had promised, eager to be out the window. I greeted him at the door with anxiety.

"Listen Boris, you don't really want to do this. Don't be a meshugana. Tell the police. I'm sure they have acrobatic people who do this sort of thing every day. Go home to Maxi. Appreciate life while you have it."

"I have to find the statue before the police do. I told you that."

"But you didn't tell me why."

He didn't respond, just started up the stairs to our bedroom and I followed, helpless, wordless, gesticulating. He tiptoed past the bed and gazed out over the rooftops that connected our building very nicely to Veronique's. All he had to do was open the window and step out onto the roof below, which was why we always kept the window closed, and after that all he had to do was become a tight rope walker, or a cat burglar to get over the adjoining sloped roofs to the back of batiment B.

"Boris, don't do it."

He said nothing as he quietly raised the window and stepped out onto the roof below. I watched, terrified as he climbed up higher on his hands and knees and edged toward Veronique's building. He slipped and slid a bit making noise that only I heard because of the rock music from one of the buildings facing the courtyard.

I couldn't watch, and I couldn't not watch. Then he was out of sight. I shivered in spite of the heat, and got back in bed before Sol, sensing I wasn't beside him, climbed out of his deep valley of sleep and up the mountaintop of awakeness.

I bit my fingernails, which I rarely do, as I waited. I kept getting out of bed and looking out the window hoping to see Boris. But he never came and I was afraid the loud thumps of my heart would miraculously awaken the unawakable Sol.

I almost jumped out of my skin when I heard the doorbell ring.

It was Boris, to my everlasting relief. He came up with me to the bedroom and sat down on the bed. I looked at him through the blur of tears of relief.

"Hey Goldie, I'm okay. It wasn't so bad as it looked. I might even take it up as a profession."

"You took so long I was sure you had fallen and were lying all broken up somewhere. I was thinking, poor Maxi. And it would have been all my fault."

"I fell only once, and only a few feet. What took so long was finding the statue."

"You found it?"

"What's left of it. It's a sodden mess."

"Did it tell you what you wanted to know?"

"It sure did. Thank God I found it and not the police. I shoved it down between two buildings."

"What did you learn?"

"I can't tell you. The less you know the safer you'll be."

"Boris!" I yelled, then put my hand over my mouth.

"Boris?" Sol was sitting up in bed, a wild, glazed look in his eyes."

"Go downstairs quick, I'll come in a minute," I hissed. As Boris left the room, I turned my attention to Sol.

"It's all right honey, you're having a nightmare. Go back to sleep." His head was back on the pillow. He was falling back down to the bottom of the canyon.

"Solly?"

"Mnn."

"I know you're asleep, but I also know you can hear me. Don't worry and don't wake up. I can't sleep. I'm just going downstairs for a while to read. Solly?"

I got no response. I joined Boris in the living room.

"With a husband like that you could have affairs in the same bed and he wouldn't know it."

"Thanks for the advice, but Sol and I don't have affairs. And if I did it would be with a much younger man."

"Touché. Are you ready to tell me what you've been keeping from me?"

I was weary and vulnerable from my recent fright. I agreed. "Okay. But first I want to make a deal. I tell you what I know, and you tell me why it was so important for you to find the statue before the police did"

"It's a deal."

So I told him. "The day after Veronique's murder, there was a big hullabaloo in the street. I was looking out of the window. During the worst of it I saw someone—a man, or a woman dressed like a man, I can't be sure which—take a large shopping bag out from under the clochard. It happened so fast I don't think anyone else noticed. I didn't know he was dead. I only found out later when the police came and cleared out the people and turned the clochard over."

An expression came over Boris' face. It wasn't relief at finding out something important. It was more like a kind of feverish excitement.

"Could you recognize her if you saw her again?"

"Not yet. I couldn't see her face. But there was something familiar about the way she moved—if it was a she. But I have to say again—I'm not absolutely sure about that. I'm working on it. Your turn."

He swallowed and forced himself to talk. "I'm putting my trust in you. What I tell you is in strict confidence."

"I'm not a blabbermouth as you should know by now."

"Well, here goes. I have a theater group that performs for a month every year in St. Petersburg, you know that. We transport the scenery, props and costumes by truck. We've never had problems at the border either way. Not that we ever did anything wrong, but you know how those Russians are. This time one of the drivers was new so I was a little nervous.

"I was also edgy because I was approached by a Russian I knew from an old business deal that didn't work out. He wanted me to transport priceless stolen objects to a client in Paris. But he didn't tell me what the objects were or who would be receiving them."

"You refused?"

"Of course I refused. I also promised him I wouldn't report him to the Russian authorities, and I didn't. Who wants a run-in with these gangsters? I thought that ended it."

"It didn't?"

"After I got back to France I was approached by a man I knew, a member of the Russian Federal Security Service, formerly known as the KGB. He accused me of transporting three small priceless paintings. I denied it. I didn't tell him about the proposition made by my former business associate. I go to Russia a lot and I didn't want to be on the mafia hit list.

I let him search the van. He found nothing, but he told me if I didn't locate and recover the paintings I was in real trouble. Former KGB men can be tough. I was a piece of meat sandwiched between the Mafia and the Russian Feds.

Later, when I looked at the inventory, I discovered, with a sinking feeling, that a hollow papier mache statue was missing—just the right size to hold the paintings—a statue we called Bathsheba because it looked like a Rembrandt of the same name.

"I had to find it to make absolutely sure that it was mine, that I had transported the paintings. I had to destroy the evidence before the police could find it and connect me to the murders. Do you understand now, Goldie?"

"I understand you lied to me, Boris. You lied to me about a lot of things."

"I lied and I have no excuses."

"Good. So the statue contained priceless paintings?" I said, "That explains a lot. If Jacques and Arnaud were in on this together, is it possible that Jacques could have been your driver?"

"Sure. I don't know what he looked like, that picture in the newspaper showed only part of his profile, not enough to tell, but it sounds plausible," Boris said.

"Who could have hired them? And who could have hired the clochard?" I wondered out loud.

"Maybe it was the same person," Boris said. "Maybe there was a double cross."

"Right. The person who hired Arnaud to pick up the paintings from Jacques probably found out Arnaud had sold out to the Russian authorities and decided to dump him and hire the clochard to do the job instead. The Russian who was in the cellar with Arnaud could have been your Russian agent. Jacques could have been murdered because no one told him about the change in plans. No one told him to expect the clochard instead of Arnaud. He must have put up a struggle against this interloper."

"Not bad," Boris said.

"But where does Veronique fit in? She knew nothing about the paintings."

"You tell me, you're the one who's been figuring things out."

"My mind isn't functioning any more. I'm exhausted. Listen Boris, don't tell Sol any of this. He's worried enough about me as it is."

"Of course not. The same goes for Maxi. Unfortunately I have to go back to Russia in a few days to organize next year's season and I don't mind telling you, Goldie, I'm scared shitless."

"I guess you can't go to the police."

"No. I've been warned to keep my mouth shut by the ex KGB man. The Russians play hard ball."

"Was he the man I saw you coming out of the art gallery with?"

"Yes. Take care of yourself, Goldie. I'll be back as soon as I can."

"You too, I wouldn't want to be in your Nikes."

CHAPTER TWENTY-ONE

I talked to Maxi on the phone next morning. She told me she had sold six paintings at her vernissage, with three possibilities. Not bad. I was pleased to hear she was no longer mad at me, but after another sleepless night it was my turn to be cranky with her. She paid no attention. She told me Boris had been out all night, but not to worry, it wasn't the first time.

I worried. But I kept my mouth shut. She knew nothing about Boris' run-in with the Russian Mafia and the former KGB man. He didn't want her to know—at least that's what he told me. I wasn't going to violate his trust. But I knew for sure Boris wasn't out for a night's fling with a woman and I was fearful for him.

All I knew was that the Russians held Boris responsible for the theft of the paintings. They had ordered him to find them—or else. That "or else" terrified me.

I couldn't just sit around and let things happen. I had to try to find out more about the paintings and where they were. Who could I talk to? Sylvie? She seemed to know everything that was going on in the neighborhood. But lately, every time I saw her on the street she cut me dead. Maybe that was because I was the last person to see Veronique alive, or so the newspapers said. Maybe Sylvie didn't want to dirty her reputation by associating with me. Or maybe she thought I was the murderer and she might be my next victim.

I suddenly remembered that her TV had been off the night before for the second time in the history of my life on rue Abbe Etienne. The first time was the night Jacques was murdered and she was at an all-night recording session. I was glad she wasn't home or she might have seen Boris doing his cat-burglar number on the roofs below. Maybe someone else had. But if I knew my neighbors, they would soon as not shut their eyes to such shenanigans, as long as it didn't impinge on their lives.

Who else was there to talk to? Dimitri? Was it safe to confide in him? He was the sweetest guy in the world, but that didn't mean anything. All sorts of unlikely people were getting woven into this tapestry of murder. Was he a golden thread? He had pictures of Veronique all over his apartment. Why? Was I a fool to trust him?

Sol was up now and shaved. He was hanging around the apartment in his pajama bottoms looking lost, the angry rash clawing at his neck to the north and his ankles to the south. I sat at the table drinking coffee and trying to solve three murders.

Sol was hanging around because he was determined not to let me out of his sight. Two shadows I didn't need.

"Listen Sol. Go to the library. Do your research. Stop worrying about me."

"Every time I walk out of the house and leave you by yourself, you get into trouble."

"I promise to behave. Besides, I can't stand looking at that rash. If you don't put your clothes on and walk out the door with your papers, you'll be surprised at what I'm capable of doing."

"Okay, okay. Have it your way. But I take no responsibility for the consequences."

So he left me alone with my thoughts, which returned to Dimitri. I decided to go and see him and hear what he had to say. He had lived in the neighborhood a long time, for whatever that was worth.

I rang his bell and was buzzed in.

Pascal greeted me looking sleepy in his pajamas and rubbing his eyes. At ten a.m.? Then I remembered Dimitri's late hours.

Pascal said, "Papa dort."

"Puis, je vais chez moi."

"No Madame, j'ai faim." He took my hand and led me to the kitchen. Why was he still here? I was under the impression he had been sent to his mother's aunt in the country.

The kitchen was a dream. Modern and old-fashioned at the same time. A wood beam ceiling, a large stone fireplace, blue Spanish tiles on the walls and counters, a dark wood table, and all the latest kitchen equipment.

"Je voudrais chocolat, s'il vous plait, Madame," he said.

I took a container of milk out of the refrigerator and put it in a pot on the stove, then found a box of powdered cocoa on the shelf. Pascal took some old pieces of baguette out of a cloth bag and put them on the table. The jam and butter were already there. A pretty crummy breakfast for a growing kid. I thought of my own adult children with a pang. I was crazy about those turkeys even though I was neglecting them. To me they were the cat's meow, and so were my peerless grandchildren. I felt guilty and I missed them. Maybe Pascal was getting the affection I was too far away to bestow on my own. Not true. A piece of my heart was already owned by this small, big-eyed kid with that mop of raven hair.

As I was stirring the powder into the warm milk, Dimitri came in yawning and hiking up his maroon silk pajama bottoms. He looked surprised, but not too surprised to be welcoming.

"Good morning, Goldie, I was just thinking about you."

"Good morning, Dimitri, I'm flattered."

"I've been thinking about hiring a nanny for Pascal. May I offer you the job?"

"I'd rather be a doting aunt, and visit him at my own convenience. By the way, are you still taking him to Veronique's aunt?"

"No. While Pascal is having breakfast we can talk in the studio."

"Good."

I sat on Dimitri's chair in front of the table, while he pushed aside some pieces of cloth and sat on the table. It was a strange reversal, looking into my own apartment. I could also see into Sylvie's living room, which was just slightly below Dimitri's.

"I changed my mind about taking Pascal to Veronique's aunt. I couldn't let him go." There was a long pause, then he said, "Pascal is my son."

I was speechless, which is unheard of. It was the last thing I expected to hear. And yet, Pascal had called him Papa.

"Veronique was living with Arnaud. She wanted a child. She couldn't have one with him. She asked me to be the father and I agreed. I loved Veronique, not in that way, of course, and I liked the idea of being a father.

"She thought Arnaud would understand. She was wrong. He beat her brutally." His voice was tense. "I wanted to kill him. I didn't know I had that much hatred in me. Lucky for him he disappeared before I could get to him. I haven't seen him since, and I hope I never do."

Neither of said anything for a moment, then I took courage.

"I hate to tell you, but Arnaud Duvier is back in Paris."

A look of hatred transformed his face. "Are you sure?"

"Sylvie said she saw him. And Veronique told me it was Arnaud and a Russian stranger who kept her prisoner in the cellar of the gallery. Didn't she tell you?"

"No. She must have been afraid of what I would do if I found out. So that's why she had those terrible bruises on her face."

While he tried to control his emotions, I stood up and looked out of the window. I wanted to know if Dimitri could see the corner where the clochard had slept. Of course he couldn't, it was on the same side of the street and hidden.

I took a deep breath, turned to him and asked, "Do you remember the night after Jacques was murdered, there was a fight on the street?"

His face had relaxed, but a certain intensity remained in his eyes as he answered. "Yes, but I have the ability to block things out that interfere with my work."

"But you had to take a break sometime. When you did, did you look out of the window?"

"I suppose so. Once or twice."

"Did you notice anything out of the ordinary?"

"Out of the ordinary? Very little is ordinary on this street."

"Yes, but try to remember."

He thought for a moment. "You mentioned Sylvie. I think it was that same night that I saw her through the window wearing a man's coat, shoving her hair up into a baseball cap."

Sylvie! Of course! I flashed through my mental files and came up with pictures of Sylvie—the way she moved that last time I had tea with her. The movements matched up with the woman in man's clothes who took the shopping bag from under the Clochard.

So it was Sylvie! And it must have been Sylvie who had given the clochard poisoned wine. Or was it?

"You look very pale, Goldie. Don't worry about her. It wasn't so unusual. Sylvie often dresses in men's clothes at night."

I tried to stop my jaw from shaking. I had come too close to something and I didn't know what to do with it.

I focused on a painting on the wall. It was a beautiful little still life in oil, almost in the style of a Courbet. Dimitri saw me looking at it.

"My brother Alexi was a painter."

"You have a brother?"

"Yes. But he no longer paints. He's been a novice monk for seven years. In two days he'll take his vows, then he'll be completely lost to me."

"I'm sorry." I suddenly felt frightened. I couldn't explain it. I had to get out of there.

"I'm going now. Sorry I bothered you and Pascal so early."

As Dimitri said goodbye he looked strange, as though he had entered an alien world and locked the door behind him.

When I got home Sol was talking on the telephone. "Boris," he hissed.

"Give it to me. I have to talk to him." I grabbed the phone out of his hand. "Listen Boris I found out…"

"I can't talk, I have to go or I'll miss my plane."

"Listen…"

He hung up.

Sol said, "Boris said to tell you his plans had changed and he's leaving for Russia immediately. He's lucky he got a seat."

"I have to talk to him now! What am I going to do?"

"You'll figure something out."

That was all the sympathy I got from Sol. But then he knew nothing of the earthquake I had just experienced, or of the necessity to tell Boris that it was Sylvie who had taken the paintings.

After a few minutes I calmed down. What else could I do? I felt relief that Boris hadn't disappeared. But I wasn't too happy that he was on his way to Russia, a minnow among sharks.

CHAPTER TWENTY-TWO

I poked around in the cupboard and found a can of Campbell's chicken noodle soup I had bought in the underground supermarket. It wasn't home-made, but in moments of duress a bowl of any kind of hot chicken soup gives me comfort nothing else can.

"Goldie, soup in the summer?"

"And why not? Want some?"

"No thanks. I'll have a baguette with a little leftover chicken liver."

"Pate forestier."

"Whatever."

As I was washing the dishes, I heard the downstairs buzzer. I dried my hands and picked up the intercom receiver. It was Dimitri. I looked at Sol nervously.

"Don't just stand there, Goldie, invite him up. Some day you'll tell me how you really met him."

I felt embarrassed in front of my own husband. I quickly finished the dishes while Dimitri climbed the five flights.

I introduced the two men and offered Dimitri coffee. He politely declined.

"Sit down, make yourself comfortable," I told him. He sat down on the edge of our sofa while Sol looked him over. Except for the blond pony tail I could see that Sol approved. He made quick judgments that were usually accurate.

We chatted about this and that, but I knew he had a special reason for coming to see me that he didn't want to talk about in front of Sol. I guess Sol sensed it too.

"If you folks will excuse me, I have to get back to the library before the line gets too long." He didn't seem worried about leaving me alone with Dimitri as he got up, took a couple of notebooks off the table and put them in his worn leather attaché case.

"Sol's writing a book and has to do research."

"That's right. You guys have a nice chat. I'll see you later."

When Sol was gone, Dimitri came right out with it.

"I need to ask a favor of you—your husband also, if he's willing. But I wanted to talk to you about it first."

"I'm listening."

"Tomorrow I go to the South of France. My brother will be initiated into the Benedictine order."

"You told me. Congratulations. Is that the appropriate thing to say?"

"Not really. I've been trying to talk him out if it. I'll give it one last try. I don't think I'll succeed. If not I want to be with him for the ceremony. I want him to know that I love him, even though I can't approve his decision."

"So how can I help?"

"Will you come with me and take care of Pascal? It's a lot to ask, but there's no one else I trust, and he's very fond of you."

"Of course I'll go with you. It will be a pleasure looking after Pascal. Sol will have to decide for himself." I felt excited by the prospect of seeing a different aspect of French life. "Will I be allowed to attend the ceremony? Are agnostics welcome?"

"Yes, surely. It will take place in an ancient abbaye in the peaceful countryside of Aquitaine."

"How long will we be there?"

"Only two nights. But we have to leave early tomorrow morning.

"I'll talk to Sol, but I doubt he'll come. He doesn't enjoy traveling. I don't think he'll mind my going away for two days. But I'll go even if he does. So that's settled."

Dimitri was in much better spirits when he left.

Sol did mind.

"It's only two nights," I told him.

"Do as you like."

The next morning Dimitri and Pascal and I were in Montparnasse station boarding the TGV, a fast train that would take us South. I looked forward to learning more about the culture of my adopted country. That ought to please Maxi who was always bugging me about my lack of knowledge. I would also learn something about an alien religion, as alien to me as my own.

In our comfortable seats we sailed past the outskirts of Paris and into unfamiliar countryside. I was lulled into semi-sleep by the smooth rhythm of wheels against track. At moments I would awaken to see cows or goats in fields, I couldn't tell which, because of the speed of the train.

We had seats facing each other with a table between. Pascal was next to me, sleeping with his head on my lap, poor lamb. I wasn't much of a substitute for his mother.

At Bordeaux I staggered out of the train in that woozy state I enter when I finally sleep after not sleeping. In Bordeaux I thought I saw my shadow, but I couldn't be certain, the station was so crowded. Just the thought that he might be there shook me awake. I was on the alert as Pascal and I followed Dimitri to another platform where our rinky-dink connection waited for us. Was it also waiting for my shadow?

I didn't see him as I entered the train or watched the platform from my seat. He wasn't there, but my anxiety remained. The train started. It was an ancient affair that trundled along like a baby taking his first steps, or an oldster taking his last.

I was awake on this leg of the journey—the hard seats didn't encourage snoozing. Dimitri was preoccupied with thoughts about his brother, I assumed. Pascal was reading a book. At the tender age of six when most children choose picture books, he was reading small print.

I looked out of the window at a forest of tall skinny pine trees whose naked trunks might have been nibbled clean by giraffes, leaving greenery shaped like Chinese hats on the top. After the forest came fields of sunflowers. And after the sunflowers, more forests.

I was getting uncomfortable with the silence, but what to say? I smoothed down stray hairs on Pascal's forehead.

"How come you and your brother have Russian names, Dimitri?"

He turned away from the window. "I wish I knew. I wish I knew who our parents were. Maybe they were Russian or maybe they liked Russian names. Ours are on the list of acceptable French names, so there's no way to tell. I know nothing of my family history, except that I was born in France and I'm a Catholic. The people who looked after us when we were small made sure we had a religious education. For our worldly training, we were sent to boarding school in England."

"That accounts for your accent."

"I long ago stopped trying to find out who our parents were. Alexi knows, but he refuses to tell me. I still get a substantial monthly check from the trust. Alexi no longer does—not since he became a novice monk."

"Your brother must be very religious."

"I am not sure about that. There are other reasons for entering a monastery. Alexi was a brilliant artist. He could do anything with a brush and a little paint. He was beginning to have a successful career when he made the mistake of showing at Arnaud Duvier's gallery. Being associated with Arnaud almost ruined his reputation."

"Is that why he became a monk?"

"No. Alexi finally got out of the contract and began showing in good galleries. His career was soaring when he gave it all up and entered the Benedictine Monastery. I will never forgive myself for letting him go."

"But it was his choice. Why should you want to keep him from following his calling?"

"It wasn't his choice."

I shut up. I was butting into something that wasn't my business. I looked out at the sunflowers slowly fading past.

We got off at a small station in the sticks.

Gregory was there to meet us in an old, black Citroen. Dimitri introduced him as the caretaker of his chateau—the man who had taken care of him and Alexi when they were children.

He was ancient and very tall, with the profile of the man dancing with La Goulu in the Toulouse Lautrec painting. His eyes were almond-shaped ice slivers in a frozen face. His face didn't change as he shook our hands, bowed and held doors for us.

We bumped along country roads for about twenty minutes until we came to a long driveway that led to a castle—a castle of grey stone, and turrets and all that stuff. It was surrounded by a well tended park with vast lawns and gardens.

"This is my ancestral home, and Alexi's, though we're seldom here."

"Some home! A mausoleum."

"Gregory and Jeannine are the caretakers. A young woman comes several times a week to dust, and helps out when she's needed. It's a perfect place for weddings. But there won't be any. At least not until Pascal grows up. Perhaps then the old place will come to life."

As we got out of the car, a large yellow dog trotted over to Pascal, his tail fanning the air. The two of them eyed each other, then raced toward the huge wooden door of the castle. As I watched them, I thought-Pascal should be living in country—he needs fresh air and exercise. But not here, not under the care of a cadaver like Gregory. Why should I dislike someone at first sight? I wondered.

The old man was strong in spite of his age. He carried all the luggage as though it weighed nothing. We walked into a large entry hall with a black and white harlequin floor where an old woman was waiting for us. She was angular and dry, with strands of red woven into her gray hair. She barely responded to the kisses of Dimitri and Pascal.

French Gothic, I thought, looking at the old couple. All they needed to complete the evocation of the Benton painting was a pitchfork. I could see why Dimitri wanted me to look after Pascal during his stay.

"This is Jeannine."

I shook her hand.

She asked if I wanted to eat. I didn't. I was too tired from the train ride.

I followed Gregory up the marble staircase while Dimitri and Pascal remained below. The white banister was cold to the touch. The upstairs foyer led to a hall with closed doors on one side and floor-to-ceiling windows on the other. On the remaining walls were etchings and watercolors similar to those I had seen in Dimitri's house in Paris.

It felt creepy to be alone with Gregory in that remote section of the castle. I was relieved when he opened an ordinary looking door and motioned me into a bedroom, not a torture chamber.

The walls were patterned green silk, so was the bedspread on the canopied four-poster bed, and the curtains on the floor-to-ceiling window. Gregory pushed aside the curtains and opened the window to a huge magnolia tree with white blossoms the size of faces. Their scent floated in and made me a little dizzy. He showed me the modern tile bathroom with an American shower, then bowed and left.

When I came out of that glorious shower, I saw a plate of sandwiches and a pot of tea on the desk. I was wide awake now and hungry. I ate the sandwiches to the sound of cow bells in the fields beyond the magnolia tree.

CHAPTER TWENTY THREE

Pascal was sitting on the marble floor in the entry hall of the castle, patting a tiny, brown, furry thing. When he saw me, he let go of it and it flew to the ceiling. I swallowed a howl. I consider myself unusually brave, but I cannot cope with certain species of creatures, like bats. I made a mental note to ask Dimitri to search my room from top to bottom before I went to sleep that night, and then close the window. Dimitri came in through the front door.

"Don't mind the bats. They're harmless. They were playmates for Alexi and me when we were small. Are you comfortable in your room?"

"I should say."

"Sorry I don't have time to show you around. I'll be away for a few hours. Do you think you and Pascal can find enough to do while I'm gone?"

"Why not?"

"If you need anything, ask Jeannine. I'll show you the library."

After explaining the valuable chotchkas in the glass fronted cabinets he left us to explore the shelves of tightly squeezed books reaching up to the ceiling. I found a book of New Yorker cartoons, but couldn't concentrate on them. I needed to walk after that long train ride.

I roused Pascal out of an ancient yellowing picture book and led him through the dining room, past the marble foyer and into the salon. Old paintings looked down at us from high up on the walls. Were they Dimitri's ancestors?

We got no further, Pascal had seen the yellow dog through the window and ran outside. I followed, and while they were getting acquainted, I explored the grounds—never losing sight of him. I wished I had a pad and charcoal to sketch the happy pair.

My mood changed to anxiety as I looked up at a high window of the castle. There, in the shadow of a dark curtain, I saw Gregory watching me. Then he was gone leaving an empty space in the window and an uneasy sensation in my gut. I looked at Pascal. He was blissful. I was determined not to let him out of my sight, even for a minute.

"Let's take a walk," I said in French

"With the dog?"

"Of course."

By the time Dimitri returned, thoughts of Gregory were on hold, which did wonders for my mood. Pascal and I were snug on the couch in the library, our feet tucked under us, reading. This cozy domestic scene didn't seem to have any effect on the melancholy mood Dimitri had brought in with him. I tried to start a conversation, but gave up as we drank from the small goblets of floc Gregory brought.

Silence was still hovering while we ate on the polished oval table, now covered with a starched white cloth in the fancy dining room. The crystal chandelier hanging above us cast a dim light. On either side huge bouquets of flowers from the castle gardens decorated the fireplaces.

Arlette, the young woman who came twice a week to dust and vacuum, put plates of food in front of us. She was very shy and pretty with her hair cut in what we used to call a boyish-bob. The food was delicious, but Dimitri's unhappy silence encouraged me to drink more wine than I was used to.

After dinner we were served Armagnac in the library. I drowned the strong taste in orange juice, to Gregory's obvious disdain. Dimitri cheered up enough to give us a tour of the chateau, sprinkled with humorous stories. I have to admit I was so soused my mental camera didn't work, so I can't tell you much about the various rooms. I hoped the camera wouldn't rust from the amount of wine I drank. Wherever Dimitri led us I could smell magnolia blossoms through my alcoholic haze.

I hardly remember how I got up the stairs and into bed. But I had a great night's sleep. If there was a bat in the room I didn't know about it.

The next morning I was full of energy for the first time in days. Maybe it was the unpolluted air, or maybe it was the wine.

I sat down at the place set for me in the cozy family dining room. The others had already eaten. There was a bowl in front of me and a basket of toasted baguette pieces. Arlette entered noiselessly and poured coffee in the bowl. She looked nervous and didn't seem to understand as I tried to exchange pleasantries. Maybe it was shyness, or maybe she was afraid of something. She left quite abruptly.

I took a sip of my coffee. It seemed odd drinking out of a bowl but I guess that's the custom in France. I put creamy butter on a piece of toasted baguette and looked out the window while I chewed. Pascal was playing with the dog. I was sure the lazy-looking critter would rather be basking in the sun, but out of kindness obliged this loving alien who had dropped into its life.

I was startled out of my reverie by Dimitri. He asked if I wanted a tour of the castle grounds. I certainly did. We were joined by Pascal and the dog as we walked through the formal gardens of shaved shrubs and manicured roses. I tried to ignore Arlette who was dusting the window sills of the salon. I tried not to look at Jeannine whose laser eyes burned the flesh on my bare shoulders as she appeared and disappeared in castle windows. Dimitri showed us the kitchen garden with its vegetables and raspberries and flowers. We strolled among the cows in the fields behind the castle and in the vineyards. All the while Dimitri was fading away until he became lost to us, a wanderer in his own private thoughts.

After an early lunch Dimitri told us he had to leave, but would be back in time to take us to his brother's ordination in the Abbaye.

In the library, as Pascal and I were deciding what to do, Arlette appeared in jeans and tee shirt. Her casual clothes did nothing to relieve her anxiety. She said Dimitri wanted her to take us to the outdoor market in a nearby town to buy produce they didn't grow in the garden. I didn't want to upset her more by accepting. On the other hand with Dimitri and Arlette gone, we'd be alone in the castle with Gregory and Jeannine. That thought gave me a moment of anxiety. Oh well, it was a large castle and we ought to be able to find a private corner.

Arlette seemed relieved when I refused her invitation, and was quickly gone. But the French Gothic couple remained. Though they weren't visible I could still feel their presence, those eyes watching us? Was there something sinister they didn't want us to see? As we wandered through the museum like rooms we could hear the music of muffled footsteps following us.

I stopped and yawned and suggested loudly to Pascal that it was time for his nap. He objected, but I took his hand and led him upstairs to my room. We didn't nap. When the footsteps faded down the hallway we took off our shoes and left them under the bed. Then, on noiseless feet, we explored the upstairs rooms. We were both intrigued by a dusty old staircase that led to the attic where a garden of delights awaited us behind the door. Ancient bicycles, puppet theaters with puppets, toy trains, interested him momentarily. But the fragile old books engrossed him and he sat down to read under the light of a high window.

For me there were costumes from other centuries in chests and wardrobes—almost too fragile with age to handle. There were lots of paintings, some quite old and dusty. I picked up a beautifully rendered landscape I was sure was Alexi's. There were several Russian icons and a portrait of a lovely blond woman with intense blue eyes that looked like a Renoir. I took a dusty cloth off a small painting that looked like a Rembrandt, dark from the kind of oil he used. Could it be? It certainly looked authentic. I uncovered another painting. A Cézanne? No! Why not? If you own a castle, why not a Rembrandt and a Cézanne? But why wasn't it hanging in the salon? Maybe I'd ask Dimitri about it. I covered the paintings.

In a small glass case, I found an antique porcelain doll like the ones I coveted as a child. My childhood memories were tossed aside when I heard the sound of a car on gravel. Dimitri must be back. I looked at my watch. It was three. I remembered that we were going to the monastery that afternoon for Alexi's ordination.

We quietly left, closed the door behind us and dusted ourselves off. Then we went back to my room and put on our shoes.

CHAPTER TWENTY FOUR

We drove through a countryside of cornfields and vineyards without a word. I knew Dimitri was deeply troubled about his brother, but I was beginning to feel uncomfortable with his mood. I hadn't come all this way for the silent treatment—a punishment I didn't deserve. I had enough. So I poked my nose into his business.

"I gather you couldn't convince your brother to give up the cowl, so to speak."

"No, I couldn't. Alexi tried to explain his decision to become a monk without telling me the real reason. Each of my questions opened up another that he could not, would not answer. Then he became silent again."

"I know about silence, Dimitri, that's what I've gotten from you since we came."

"I'm sorry. There's so much that I can't express in words. But Alexi's silence is different. It's the silence of a monk. He'll never tell me anything, not about his decision, not about our parents. But we mustn't talk in front of Pascal."

"You're right. But he doesn't understand English."

"Pascal doesn't need words to understand. He is like a blind person, he can smell emotions. He can touch emotions with those little hands. We can't deceive him."

I looked at the boy. He was reading a book he'd found in the attic. I suddenly didn't want to know what it was, didn't want to know about the terrible things he'd seen and felt in his short life.

I finished my thought out loud. "Always a mother who came to him with bruises she couldn't hide with makeup. I'm sorry Dimitri. I'll shut up."

I turned my inner camera on the hilly countryside, on fields of corn shimmering on their stalks in the heat, exuding the aroma of roasting corn.

We finally drove through the gates of the monastery, which stood, on a hill like an Italian Basilica, surrounded by viridian trees, and a big cerulean sky. Dimitri parked. As we stepped out, we heard a Gregorian chant flowing through the entrance.

We were late. An usher led us through the crowded church to benches close to the ceremony, close to the swinging censer and the smoke and aroma of incense. A choir of monks and priests in beige cowls stood in a semi-circle chanting in the back. A gilt medieval book gleamed on a white cloth on a table in the front. The two initiates stood with their arms stretched out like crosses. Dimitri translated as they sang the prayer, "I offer my life to God" three times, and three times sang: "Please God do not disturb my waiting."

The Bishop, dressed in gold and crimson, with a miter and staff, chanted in Latin. Then a monk picked up the leather and gold volume from the table, opened it, held it up, and turned slowly so we could all see the medieval illuminated pages.

As the two initiates stretched out face down on the floor in front of the table, the tablecloth hid their letters with promises to God.

In that Benedictine monastery in the South of France, as I watched that mysterious Mass, I wondered why Dimitri's brother was becoming a monk.

"Alexi has taken the name Cyril," Dimitri whispered. "He's the one with the sandals." The other initiate wore black shoes that poked out from under his robe, shoes that almost dispelled the aura of mystery.

The initiates stood up and approached the Bishop like a bride and groom, and took their vows. The other new monk was given the censor of smoky incense. He swung it with such vigor and enthusiasm it barely missed the nose of the Bishop. The other monks giggled and the Bishop smiled as the host and wine were offered. Brother Cyril stood apart, his eyes on Pascal.

When the ceremony was over. Cyril and the other new monk kissed their brothers on each cheek. Afterwards they frolicked like playful little puppies, and drank what was left of the ceremonial wine. Except for Cyril.

Outside, on the lawn surrounded by stone buildings, our eyes adapted to the bright sunshine. Pascal had discovered a squirrel and was trying to coax it out of a tree. I saw brother Cyril coming toward us, slowly, like the melancholy movement of a Bach cello concerto.

As he approached, casting a shadow on the sunlight radiating from the other monks, Dimitri told me his brother had chosen to work indoors in solitude, while most of the others cultivated the earth together. The monks were allowed to speak at certain times of the day, but Brother Cyril had chosen complete silence. Brother Cyril was finished with words. His last words had been spoken to Dimitri.

He came towards us with his hood off, his hair black and shining like Pascal's. When he was close to Pascal he stopped. His tall frail body swayed a moment. Then he knelt down beside the boy and held the little face in his hands. He caressed the small replica of Veronique's face with his fingertips and kissed it. He stood up and turned to Dimitri, a momentary fire in his pale blue eyes. Then the fire went out and he turned and walked away. Buildings and trees and monks seemed to fade away from him as he walked into infinity.

"Now he knows…without my saying it. Now he knows."

"But…But…you said Pascal was your…"

"Hush, he can hear you."

I couldn't believe it. Why did Dimitri make up that crazy story about being Pascal's father?

I watched a bird circling high in the sky.

"That was a cruel way for Alexi to find out," I told him.

"I could not tell him in words. I made a promise to Veronique."

At the sound of his mother's name, Pascal looked up at Dimitri.

"I can't change anything now," Dimitri said.

"The monks seem so happy here, maybe in time Alexi will be happy also."

"In time…?"

When we got back to the chateau, there was a message from Sol.

"You can call back from your room if you want privacy," Dimitri told me.

I went upstairs and shut the door. Then I sat down on the bed and dialed my number. When Sol picked up, I was sure I heard faint breathing on the phone. Gregory?

"Goldie?"

"It's me. What's up?"

"Something funny's going on in the building next door," he told me. "I thought maybe you should know."

I was curious, but I was also nervous about the breathing on the phone. "Couldn't it wait until I get home?"

"Why? It's just that Sylvie hasn't been blasting her TV since you left. In fact she doesn't even have it on at all."

"For this you called me?"

"Well, it's just that the police are in her apartment now. I can hear them when I put my head to the wall."

"Now who's being snoopy?"

"Also, Veronique's furniture's been removed from her apartment and there's a "For Sale" sign. They probably finished the investigation and found nothing."

"They found something all right. They finally figured out what I already knew, that…" Oh God. I hoped I hadn't said too much.

"That what…?"

"I'll tell you when I get back. So where is Sylvie?"

"The rumor is that she came into a lot of money and moved to the country," Sol told me.

"It sounds reasonable."

"Why Goldie?"

I could still hear the breathing.

"Never mind. Listen we shouldn't talk on the telephone. I'll tell you when I get home tomorrow. Kiss kiss."

After dinner, with Pascal in bed, Dimitri and I went into the library. He was drinking Armagnac in a delicate stemmed glass. I abstained.

"I owe you explanations," he said.

"You don't, but I'm all ears."

"You know now that I lied about being Pascal's father."

"Everyone's entitled to a little lie when it's necessary to protect someone."

"Lies are sometimes the only way out, but they don't protect anyone. I'd like to tell you about Alexi."

"I'd like to hear it."

"Alexi had an affair with Veronique when she was still living with Arnaud. That was dangerous. Arnaud is as capable of killing as another person is of filing a nail."

"That's a pretty serious charge. If that was the case, wouldn't he be in jail now?"

"I'm not saying he's a murderer, but he's a police informer. He's too valuable to them on the streets. I don't think I need say more."

"So your brother had an affair with Veronique, and Pascal is his son, and he only learned about it today when he saw him."

"Yes."

"Why did he go into the monastery? Was he afraid of Arnaud Duvier?"

"Alexi was never afraid of anything in his life. It wasn't that, but he won't tell me the reason. I only know that he truly loved Veronique, so whatever made him run away must have been so strong and so evil that he deserted rather than involve her. But he will not tell me about it and he will not tell me who our parents were."

"Are you sure he knows?"

"He knows."

When I arrived home the next day Sol looked grim.

"I have bad news."

"Not Boris!"

"Sylvie. She was found this morning, floating in the Stravinsky Fountain, under the Niki de St. Phalle snake. The snake was stuck—spouting water on her. Her hair was tangled in the mechanism."

He handed me the newspaper. The picture had been shot from above. It was like Sol had described. You could see the stained-glass windows of St. Merri, hazy, behind the sprays of water. On her shoulder, barely noticeable, was a tattoo of a crucifix.

"I think it's time to go home to New York, Goldie."

"I'm not ready to go back. I agree only to move out of this neighborhood if we survive this business."

CHAPTER TWENTY FIVE

I slept into the afternoon. It wasn't only that I was tired from my trip, I just wasn't ready to look another day in the eye. Events were getting too heavy for my soft shoulders. Every time I woke up a spider knitting his web on the ceiling stared reproachfully at me, so I closed my eyes again and went back to sleep

Sol nudged me in late afternoon. "Goldie, I'd like to let you sleep forever, but I promised we'd go over to Maxi's for a dinner party tonight."

"You accepted? But Sol, you hate dinner parties."

"You wouldn't have to cook."

"When did I last cook?"

"Listen, I said we'd go. But if you don't want to, I'll phone and make an excuse."

"No, we'll go. I don't want to aggravate Maxi on top of everything. What time is it?"

"Relax, we've got a while."

"Is Boris back from Russia?"

"Not that I heard of."

That wasn't the answer I wanted. In the South of France I had forgotten about the Northern troubles. I forgot to worry about Boris and the former KGB man and the Russian Mafia. Now I was forced to remember.

Anyway, I got up and drank the strong coffee Sol made me, and focused on what to wear that evening. At home I usually chose the first outfit I put my hands on, but in Paris this is a big decision. I decided to give my best dress some mileage, even though it was only Maxie we were going to see. I took a look at it. It had been my best dress for twenty years and was practically new because I hardly ever wore it. But after living in the fashion capital of the world, it looked tacky, even to my untutored eye. So I chose my only nice outfit, a summer suit of ivory linen I bought in a street market for cheap.

Actually, it looked kind of nice even though I couldn't button the skirt in the back because of the croissants and had to zip it down a little so I could breathe. My sleeveless pink blouse covered the error in case I had to take my jacket off.

There were six at Maxi's when we arrived. A painter, a sculptor, and a journalist married to a printmaker. All of them would be interesting to talk to, but I don't remember if I did because guest number five was a guy so handsome I blushed to look at him. He had a great body and his features were like a movie star. Who? Maybe Robert Redford is closest. But when Maxi introduced us, he was transformed in front of my eyes into a monster by the name of Arnaud Duvier!

We had actually met once before, but at that time I hadn't seen his face because it was covered by a balaclava—but I had felt his fist in my eye—in that awful cellar under the Russian Art gallery in my building.

Guest number six was Simone. She was with Arnaud. She looked like a model wearing one of those silly designer schmattas you see on the fashion pages of the International Herald Tribune.

I couldn't tell you what the other people wore or said if you were to torture it out of me, even though for two hours I sat at the same table with them picking at Maxi's gourmet cooking. For two hours I was aware only of the hulking presence of Arnaud Duvier. His good looks, a mask covering a vicious brute. Dimitri had implied he was capable of murder. Had he murdered Veronique and Sylvie? What was he doing here? Was Maxi next? No! I wouldn't let it happen.

After dinner I tried to talk to her. Every time I got near she snapped at me. She was fussing around, chit chatting with her guests, serving cognac in swollen goblets. She refused to leave her guests to talk to me in private. I bided my time, pretending to look at paintings and books and furniture, which I already knew by heart. I finally caught her alone in the kitchen.

"Later, Goldie."

I'm pretty even tempered but I wasn't having any of that. I grabbed her arm and pulled her out of the kitchen and into the furthest bedroom. I shut the door-and got straight to the point.

"Why did you invite Arnaud Duvier?"

"That's none of your business."

"I need to know. Now! I won't let you go until you tell me. I'm little, but I'm strong!" I wasn't. She knew I wasn't.

"Okay, okay. I used to know him when he had that gallery on your street. The other day I met him by chance and on an impulse, asked him to dinner. May I be excused now?"

So even judgmental Maxi was lying. "By chance, my foot. Does Boris know you invited him?"

"That's also none of your business."

"I know you Maxi. You are not going to damn well start something up with him while Boris is away?"

"For God's sake, Goldie!"

"Listen Maxi, that schmuck is somehow mixed up in the murders in my neighborhood, and…"

"Do you have proof, Inspector Goldie?"

"What do I need proof? Suspicion should be enough to keep you away from him."

"Don't exaggerate."

"I'm not exaggerating. He brutalized Veronique when they lived together. I know that because she told me just before she was strangled and thrown into the canal."

"Abusers aren't necessarily murderers. Goldie stay out of it. I can take care of myself."

Maxi opened the door just in time for us to see Arnaud Duvier's girl-friend, Simone, going into the bathroom. Was she spying for him?

I went back into the living room and sat down. I looked at Sol. He was actually enjoying himself. He'd found a guest who spoke English and knew a little about the esoteric subject matter of his future book. When the man left, Sol suggested that it was also time for us to go home. I disagreed. I intended to stay until Arnaud Duvier walked out the door. I wasn't going to leave Maxie alone with him even if he was with Simone.

When we finally left Maxi kissed me coldly and said, "You don't have to protect me from Arnaud. If I was so inclined I could call him up and ask him to come back after you leave."

Outside, Sol asked me, "What's going on?"

"Nothing. I was just wondering if I really know Maxi."

"What does that mean?"

"It means I'm tired and I want to go home to bed."

CHAPTER TWENTY SIX

Boris phoned the next afternoon. Thank God he was back from Russia and safe. Not that it kept me from worrying, I just didn't worry as much.

"Goldie, I have to talk to you."

"So talk."

"In person."

I groaned inwardly. Boris was trouble. But trouble had become a way of life and so had Boris. And I had something to tell him that couldn't wait.

I met him in the Luxembourg Gardens in late evening when the sky held that special Paris light the Impressionists loved to paint. It was even more mysterious now, blending with late twentieth century smog. We sat on iron chairs near the pond in the disintegrating sunlight and nursed our anxieties. A broken boat wobbled on the smooth surface of the water. Neither of us wanted to start the conversation. We looked at the carefully arranged flower beds sprinkled with sounds of children playing. A child's striped ball rolled toward my feet. I picked it up and put it into the outstretched arms of a small boy.

I suggested we walk to the Seine. With a grunt, Boris got up. We wandered through the gardens, past the Senat and into the street, where the buildings were blanched and turning pink from reflected sunset.

I was trying to keep up with him and panting from the effort. "You made a million dollars on your deal in Russia?"

"Don't be funny. I didn't have the chance to conduct business. You don't conduct business from a Russian jail."

"What?"

"Of course I wasn't tortured like I might have been in the old days."

"What are you talking about?"

"They put me in jail overnight. One of those stinking Russian holes left over from Stalin's days of glory."

"Why?"

"For transporting Russian paintings out of the country."

"But you didn't…knowingly…"

"Not knowingly. I didn't even know for sure until I found what was left of the statue on the roof outside Veronique's apartment."

"Couldn't you convince the Russians you were just a dupe?"

"Sure. I convinced them but it didn't make any difference. What was important to them, innocent or not, was that my truck brought the stolen paintings into France. That dumped the problem into my lap."

"What does that mean?"

"It means they want me to know I am in serious trouble and I better find the paintings yesterday. I'm temporarily in their employ. Can you imagine? Me, a Russian agent!"

I had to laugh. Boris could single-handedly screw up the entire Russian secret service—if it wasn't already screwed up.

"I work for them without pay." Boris told me, "I have to find the paintings or else I'm fed to the wolves of the Steppes—their brothers in the mafia."

"Thank God they let you go."

"I'm a French citizen. They didn't want an international incident if they could help it."

"What kind of paintings would fit into that Goddamned statue I wish I had never seen."

"Small paintings—stolen from where? They wouldn't tell me. Maybe the vaults in the Hermitage. Incredibly valuable. But they also wouldn't tell me what they were. They didn't want to make it too it easy for me."

"How could someone steal paintings from a famous museum like that?"

"In Russia, Big Brother is no longer watching."

"He's watching you."

He ignored the remark. We had reached the Seine and stopped to look at the water. He seemed to be counting the sparkles of light on the river which were temporarily displaced by a passing Bateau Mouche. He turned to look at me, examining my face.

I put my hand up to my cheek. "What, what? Is my lipstick smeared?"

He laughed a little. It wasn't the hearty laugh you could expect from the Boris of old. "I was just thinking…My sister neglected to tell me about the change in drivers. I guess she didn't know how sinister it would turn out to be. And even if she had told me, I probably wouldn't have known that Jacques, the new driver, was a plant—that he would be transporting stolen paintings in our truck and bringing them to his apartment for Arnaud to pick up."

I added, "Or that the plans would be changed at the last moment because Arnaud double-crossed whoever, and the clochard was hired to replace him."

"Now I merely have to find out who hired Jacques and Arnaud, and, more importantly, where the paintings are, then get them to the Russians. A piece of cake."

Irony from Boris? I suddenly had the horrible thought that it might be Boris' sister! Who was better situated to receive stolen paintings? No it wasn't possible!

We walked past Shakespeare and Co.—no longer the establishment of Sylvia Beech who had published James Joyce when no one else would. But today was today, and Sylvia Beech and her book shop were long gone.

We walked past the boarded up old-book stands, and then crossed over the bridge to Notre Dame. The skateboarders were packing up their paraphernalia and executing a few last minute leaps. The hurdy-gurdy woman was near the entrance, playing and singing an ancient Breton song, her voice hoarse the way it sometimes got at the end of the day. I wondered about her, about her secret life when she was not basking in the streets. I wondered if she were a man in drag.

I looked into Notre Dame as I always did when I was with Sol. This time I saw my other neighbor, Madame Clara, kneeling, her shawl-covered head bowed in the flickering candlelight, looking forlorn. I felt guilty because I hadn't gotten around to asking her tea. Should I do it now? No, I couldn't disturb her in such a private moment.

We left her there and walked onto the bridge that attached itself to the Right Bank. On our right was a view of the prow of Ile St. Louis. We stopped at the low rail on the left and looked west where the last of the sun had turned the river red. The Hotel Dieu was mottled, and beyond that, the old prison, with it's three, pointed towers and crosses had turned from gray to pink.

"I need your help, Goldie," Boris whispered.

I was startled.

"Well that's a turnabout."

"I'm serious. The ex KGB man told me you held the key to the missing paintings."

"Me? An ex KGB man was referring to me? Me, Goldie from Jackson Heights and Greenwich Village? How could that be?"

"They have a man watching you."

"What man?"

"You know. The one who's been following you."

For a moment I didn't know who he meant. Then it hit me. "Boris, you fink, you lied to me! You said he was from the police. You said he was protecting me."

"I plead guilty of compassion. I didn't want you to be frightened."

"Damn it, Boris!"

"I'm sorry. What else can I say?"

"Oh well, I should have known by his loud clothes. A Frenchman wouldn't be seen dead in them."

"Listen, Goldie. I saw in the newspaper that your neighbor Sylvie was murdered. She must have known something or she'd still be alive. Did she tell you anything?

This was what I had come to talk to Boris about. This was what, for some reason, I had found it difficult to say to him. Now he had given me an opening.

"She knew something all right. She was the one who took the shopping bag from under the clochard."

"What?"

"That's what I tried to tell you when you hung up on me to catch the plane to Russia."

"You've known all along?"

"No I didn't. Calm down. I just found out."

"Tell me!"

"My friend Dimitri, who lives across the street from me and Slyvie, can see in her window. He told me he saw her change into man's clothes the night I saw someone take that shopping bag from under the clochard."

"I'll be damned!"

"I think the paintings were in that shopping bag."

"I think you're right. Dimitri? That dress designer? What does he know?"

"Nothing. He's totally out of it."

"Are you sure?"

"I'm sure. He had no idea of the significance of what he told me. He said Sylvie was always dressing up in men's clothes."

"Could he also have seen her take that shopping bag from under the clochard—from his window?"

"No. The clochard was on the same side of the street and around a corner."

"Did you see where Sylvie went with the bag?'

"No I couldn't. It was a mob scene."

Boris thought for a minute. "If it was Sylvie who paid the Clochard to take the paintings from Veronique's apartment, she must also have given him the poisoned wine so he couldn't talk. So who murdered her to keep her quiet?"

"That's the million dollar question. The clochard murdered Jacques, Sylvie murdered the clochard. Will Sylvie's killer be killed next? It's beginning to sound like 'The House That Jack Built.'"

Boris said, "I want to know who hired the North Africans to stage a fight as a diversion so she could take the shopping bag without being seen."

"Right. Poor Sylvie. I guess whoever it was promised her the money for her dream house in the country."

"Well, she didn't get to the country, she only got as far as the Stravinsky Fountain," Boris said.

I wouldn't be hearing her TV anymore. In a funny way, I sort of missed her—a human life was more precious than a few hours sleep. But she had poisoned that pathetic clochard, and I couldn't bring her back anyway.

"By the way, when I was prowling around on the rooftops I found a sharp kitchen knife. Nothing out of the ordinary. If the clochard cut Jacques' throat with it, that could explain why there was so much blood. I didn't touch it. I left it there."

"I wonder why the police didn't find it?"

"Maybe they weren't motivated by threats on their lives. Anyway it was hidden under a tile and I left it hidden."

It was getting dark. The apartments on the Ile de La Cite were throwing handfuls of light into the Seine.

"You're sharp, Goldie, you figured out the clochard murdered Jacques before the police did."

"I observe and remember."

"You keep a lot in that head of yours."

"In my files."

"I'll bet there are things in those file you don't even know you have. I'd go through them carefully, if I were you."

"I'll consider it."

"Sol told me you took a trip down south with your friend Dimitri. Want to share it with me?"

"No, thanks. It's confidential. And I told you before, Dimitri has nothing to do with this."

"Look, I'm the one in trouble. The Russians seem to think you have the missing puzzle pieces. I need to know everything you've gotten yourself into."

"The Russians overestimate me. You now know everything I know that has to do with the murders. If I told you about Dimitri's personal life, I'd betray a confidence. I won't do it."

We stayed a little longer and watched the Bateaux Mouches skimming over the Seine and under the Pont D'arcole. I hoped I wasn't hurting Boris, but I couldn't bring myself to needlessly drag Dimitri and Pascal into it.

I was thinking of them snug in the library of Dimitri's house when suddenly, for no reason, an image of the old hotel next door to Dimitri's house popped out of my files.

"Boris, is there any way you could you find out who owns the ancient Hotel on my block?" I asked him.

"Sure. No problem. Records are kept in the Mairies of all the arrondisements. I'll do it first thing in the morning. I also want to know."

"Good. Now I have to tell you something I don't want to tell you."

"Tell me anyway."

"Arnaud Duvier was at your house last night. I was terrified for Maxi."

"I know, I asked her to invite him. I wanted to talk to him. I wanted to find out what he knows. Arnaud will always sell himself to the highest bidder. I thought I'd be back from Russia in time. But, as you know, I was detained."

"I hope you set her straight about him. I couldn't."

"Don't worry about Maxi, she hates him."

But I worried about her as I went back to a grumpy Sol. He had Chinese take-out waiting for me. I hate eating Chinese in Paris. It can't hold a candle to what you get in New York where they throw everything in a wok and in five minutes it's a banquet. Anyway, it wasn't Chinese takeout, it was Vietnamese.

That night I lay awake for hours thinking about what Boris had said, wondering what I knew that I didn't know I knew—going through my mental files to see what I missed—to find connections.

CHAPTER TWENTY SEVEN

Sol was still put out with me next morning for spending so much time with Boris. I couldn't explain the situation without getting him involved, and I didn't want to do that. As a result, he took himself off to the library as soon as it was open and said he wouldn't come home for lunch.

I was sorry he was upset with me, but it was better than having him home, under foot, watching my every move. I needed space to sort things out. Boris had put doubts in my mind about Dimitri—had made me wonder if he was somehow involved in the murders—without knowing it, of course.

No. Arnaud Duvier held the key, and I had to find him. Not that I was so anxious to see that scum again, but I needed to talk to him. If he knew where the paintings were hidden and I could get it out of him, Boris would be off the hook. But if he did, he probably wouldn't come right out and tell me. But he might let it slip. He wasn't so smart. He had stupidly double-crossed his employer by working with the Russians, and his employer had double-crossed him by hiring Sylvie and the Clochard.

If he didn't know where the paintings were, he certainly would know who hired him. He could tell me that much. But would he? Maybe I could make a deal. But I had nothing to trade. Maybe Boris did. But Boris wasn't available at the moment. He was tracking down the owner of the ancient hotel.

Why would anyone want to steal famous paintings when they could see them in a museum? Maybe it was the power of possessing something unattainable-forbidden fruit and all that. Oh well, to each his own.

Maybe I could pry something out of Arnaud by threatening to tell the police that he was the one who had kidnapped me. No, that wouldn't work, he was a police informer and they needed him out in the street, not in jail. But how to find out where Arnaud lived? Who would know? Maxi? I called her.

"Yes, as it happens I do have Arnaud's address. His current address. It changes with his women."

"Of whom you are not now, never was and never will be one of."

"That's right."

She gave me the address and door code. It was on a swanky street. Might as well get it over with, I told myself, while the coast was clear. But I wasn't so anxious to be alone with that murderous creep—my hand went automatically to the fading mouse under my eye. Who would be willing to go with me? I couldn't think of anyone. Then I thought of Dimitri. I would ask him to come with me. I phoned him.

When he answered, I got right down to business. "I'm going to see Arnaud Duvier. Want to come along?"

"Yes! I also want to see him.

I heard the door to my apartment slam.

"Hold on, Dimitri, Sol just walked in, damn!"

"What damn?" said Sol, "I came back to clear the air. I can't stand it when there's bad feeling between us."

"Okay Sol, wait a minute." I spoke into the phone, "I have the address. Can we go now, Dimitri?."

Sol interrupted. "Go where Goldie? I came back to be with you, to make up."

"Shush, Sol." I spoke into the phone. "What will you do about Pascal? Wait! I have an idea. Sol can babysit, is that alright with you, Dimitri?"

"Yes, if your husband doesn't mind."

I put my hand over the receiver, "Listen Sol, you'll love this kid. You can teach him to play baseball. There's a back yard. You can take him to the carousel, to MacDonald's for lunch. What about it?"

"I thought you already made up my mind."

"Come on, you love kids and Pascal is a piece of cake."

"Yeah, okay. You convinced me. I'll take him to a toystore to buy a tennis ball and baseball bat. I'll make a major leaguer out of him."

"Sol, you're a peach."

A little while later we met Dimitri at his door. Pascal stood beside him. He pecked me on each cheek.

"This is uncle Sol," I told him in my own brand of French.

"Bonjour Monsieur," said Pascal. Sol picked him up with his big hands and was also pecked on both cheeks. In return, Sol gave the boy a good American bear-hug. I can tell when Sol loses his heart to someone. So we left them alone to enjoy the day together.

Dimitri and I took the Metro at Chatelet in the direction of La Defense, changed at Concorde, then got off at Solferino. I thought I saw the man who had been shadowing me, the one who had been transformed by Boris from a French cop to a Russian agent. But maybe it was my imagination. I wasn't paying much attention because I had my mind on the meeting with Arnaud and I was a little edgy.

We hadn't let him know we were coming because I wanted to catch him off guard—as long as Dimitri was with me. Dimitri was pretty husky under that delicate exterior.

We got out in front of the Orsay Museum and continued down Solferino, walking away from the Seine, turning left on rue de l'Universite. As we walked, I couldn't help admiring the elegant old buildings on a street coveted by many Parisians—and by me. Maxi could tell us the period from her days as a guide, but she wasn't there.

It was a quiet street, yet close to the pulse of the city. Living there, one could walk to the Louvre and the Pompidoux Center, and the fabulous produce market on the rue de Seine.

We pressed the code numbers and the tall black Iron gate clicked open. The large courtyard had four entrances to the building that curved around it. The nearest was the one we were looking for, and of course we had to trudge up six stories of creaky carpeted stairs.

The door to the top right apartment was opened by Simone, the woman who had been with Arnaud at Maxi's dinner party. She was surprised to see us and not very welcoming.

"What do you want?"

"We want to see Arnaud," Dimitri told her.

She started to shut the door in our faces, but changed her mind and let us in. We stepped onto a foyer floor of rough red stones. A mirror on the wall showed my messy hair and all my blemishes. I hate that. Below the mirror was a walnut dry sink, and a Chinese bowl filled with lemons.

From there we could see into the living room—all wood beams and skylights, but elegant, not like my apartment. It was a huge room with flowers on the window sills overlooking the courtyard. The walls had paintings on them, not like the junk in Arnauds former gallery turned box depository. I turned my mental camera on a Picasso, a Matisse, and a small Cezanne.

"Arnaud is not here," she snapped.

"When will he be back?" Dimitri asked.

"Never! Wait a minute."

She went into the bedroom and brought out a shabby suitcase and flung it at our feet. It broke open and men's clothes spilled out, including an elegant Figaret tie.

"When you find him give him that!"

"Where is he?" I asked in French.

"I don't know and I don't want to know. Now get out of here!"

It was then that I noticed a raw bruise under her eye.

When we left the apartment, the suitcase was still lying on the floor. Out in the street Dimitri and I looked at each other.

"What now?" I asked, trying not to feel discouraged.

Dimitri took my arm and we walked on the rue de l'Universite.

"Years ago," he said, "I had occasion to go to Arnaud's place in Clichy. It's very vivid in my mind. I think I can find it again, but it's not a very pleasant neighborhood."

"Let's go!"

"If he doesn't have that apartment anymore. Maybe someone in the neighborhood can tell us where he is."

"Okay."

"We'll take the Metro at St. Germain des Pres."

I hesitated. That was the scene of my humiliation. That was where Arnaud had dumped me out of the car. I wasn't so happy about retracing those steps, or seeing the tourists at the cafe "Aux Deux Magots," or the clochard on the church steps who had blown me a kiss.

"Isn't there a closer stop?"

"Not really."

On the Metro, a young man was playing "Bei Mir Bist du Schoen." When he had finished, I gave him ten francs for good luck.

The neighborhood around the Metro station in Clichy wore a universal shoddiness. I knew that at night it was alive with prostitutes and their customers. But most of them were sleeping now. We passed only two on the job, in mother-daughter outfits of black leather skirts and see—through tops barely covering overflowing bosoms. A fluffy little dog with a pink bow snapped at the heels of the occasional rival, but ignored the general public.

We walked beneath the shadow of the domed Sacre Coeur. Except for that, we could have been in New York. The stores could have been in Spanish Harlem, except that "Bodega" was replaced by "Epicerie" or "Boucherie."

We walked down a narrow street and then another and stopped in front of a boarded up slum building that was partially occupied. A geranium brightened a window sill under a fluttering white curtain. It was not old-dignified like on rue Abbe Etienne. It looked like it had been built in the twenties and then left to its own devices. Could this be where that elegant criminal, police informer, gigolo, woman beater lived?

"This is it," said Dimitri, his face suddenly transformed with rage. In an instant he had become a stranger.

There was no locked gate, no code of secret numbers. Anyone who wished had access to the long hall that smelled of stale urine. I held my breath for a moment, then followed Dimitri, feeling the heat of his anger that trailed after him. He stopped in front of a graffiti covered door and banged on it. There was no response. He kicked it. I was afraid he would destroy it. It opened a crack—then all the way. Arnaud, spiffily dressed, stood alone in a bare gray room between an unmade cot and a table with cheap wine on it. The only window looked out on a stone wall with over-flowing garbage cans leaning against it. The only bright spot in the room was a painting of a sweet-faced blond boy. I recognized the style.

Maxi had painted it.

Dimitri and Arnaud were looking at each other, a rope of electricity, a kind of sparking umbilical cord attached them to each other. Then it snapped, and it was Arnaud who cringed. I looked at Dimitri. His face was red with hatred. We had enough murders already. I took his arm. It felt like steel, then softened.

"Can we come in?" I asked Arnaud, trying to hold Dimitri back.

"How did you find me? Did that little bitch Simone tell you?"

"You can't keep your fists out of women's faces, can you Arnaud?"

Dimitri said in a low voice, "Simone didn't tell us. I remembered from seven years ago. Seven years ago you put Veronique in the hospital and I came here to find you, but you were gone, like a snake."

"I put Veronique in the hospital, but someone closer to you put her in the grave."

Arnaud had guts, I'll say that for him.

Dimitri grabbed his arm. "What do you mean?"

I was still holding on to him and tried to pull him back.

"Let him alone, Dimitri! Please. I'd like to sit down. I'm feeling a little woozy." It wasn't true, but I had to do something. "I'd like a glass of water."

Dimitri let go of him. Arnaud straightened his jacket and went into the kitchen. Strange things happen to the human mind in moments of severe stress. When Arnaud returned and handed me the glass of water I remembered a funny story I had once heard about two men who went into a Jewish restaurant in lower Manhattan and asked for water. One said he wanted water in a clean glass. When the waiter came back, he asked, "which one of you asked for the clean glass?"

I took the water but didn't drink it.

Sitting down on a wobbly kitchen chair, I hoped that things would cool off between the two men, two men who had loved Veronique in their own ways. We hadn't come for revenge, we had come for information, at least I had, and unless the mood changed quickly, this visit would be a disaster. I couldn't just ask who had hired him to get the paintings from Jacques. I had to ease into it. Where to start?

"Where have you been hiding yourself all these years?" I asked.He turned to me with a bitter little laugh and sat down on the bed.

"I was in New York, In Queens, living with a cousin. I found a job driving a gypsy cab. That's how I learned all there is to know about America."

"Is that so?"

"Sure. I used to make a couple of hundred bucks taking tourists from Kennedy to the Waldorf."

"You're a fast learner."

"I am. I learned a New York cab driver didn't need to know the streets, he only needed a map and a spiel."

"I guess your spiel was all about crime in France."

"Right. I didn't know much at first, but I did research at the Forty-Second street library and became an expert."

He had a sense of humor, I'll say that for him. Dimitri said nothing. He seemed to be meditating.

"You'd be amazed how many Americans are in love with a Paris they've never known and never will. A Paris that never existed—a Paris of romance. They tipped me well for my lies. When it rained I made a fortune…all those wet socialites dripping outside the opera."

I laughed at the image in spite of myself. I knew now what made Arnaud so attractive beside his looks. He knew instinctively what was irresistible to each woman and exploited his knowledge. With me it's a sense of humor.

But he wasn't attractive for long. He turned to Dimitri and snarled, "Seven years ago your brother stole the only woman I ever loved."

The only woman he ever loved indeed! What a load of crap-who did he think he was, Paul Henried lighting two cigarettes and handing one to Bette Davis in "Now Voyager?" Arnaud took off his jacket, threw it on the bed and picked up a sewing kit from the table. I noticed that the cuffs of his designer shirt were frayed. I suddenly felt sorry for this pathetic, awful man, this predator in his fancy jacket and threadbare shirt—this low-life in a hovel, hiding out from the Russian secret service. But then I remembered the bruised and swollen face of Veronique and my pity evaporated.

As Arnaud reached for his jacket, I saw the small blue tattoo above his wrist. It was the same tattoo I had seen on the arms of Jacques and Veronique and in the picture of Sylvie floating in the Stravinsky Fountain. He noticed me looking, pulled down his sleeve, and sat down. He threaded the needle and started darning a frayed button hole on his designer jacket. His face lost its sneer. It looked…like the face of the little boy in the painting on the wall.

He turned to me with a strange, hollow look in his eyes. "She put that tattoo on all our arms—all five of us."

"Who?" said Dimitri.

He didn't answer the question. "She was obsessed with religion—a screwy sort of religion-out of place in a bordello."

"A bordello?" I said.

"I was ten years old when she picked me up off the streets. Veronique was a lot younger—I loved her even then. I just wanted to be with her. But Sylvie was always around, always hanging on me, the bitch. Because she was older, she thought she could have me. Then there was that sniveling little Michel who always got beaten by the Madame's lover, that big sadistic brute. Michel was so starved for love, he endured everything just to be touched. All of us were initiated into those unspeakable rites to satisfy the sexual appetites of French society—and the Madame's bank account."

I was shocked.

"Who ran this bordello?" I asked.

"A certain famous Madame who specialised in everything anybody wanted. She even had a prostitue of the troisieme age. She gave it up years ago and retired, and threw us back in the street, damaged goods. But we were adolescents by then, and we had learned a little about survival, except for Michel who ended up on the street, living in filth. That life wasn't for me. I was too smart." His smile was ironic.

I had a sudden vision of the dead clochard. Was he the pathetic Michel? I felt cold.

I heard Dimitri ask, "Who is this evil Madame?".

"A mad woman filled with delusions. She still has power and the tentacles of an octopus. My life isn't worth much at the moment. But if I tell you who she is, it won't be worth anything at all."

He snapped the sewing thread with his teeth, put on his jacket and looked into a piece of broken mirror on the wall.

"Enough of your unhappy childhood, who hired you to take the paintings from Jacques," I said.

He looked surprised. "If the Russians haven't got that out of me, what makes you think you can?"

I needed to take another tack. I looked at the painting on the wall.

"Is that you?"

"Yes?"

"Maxi painted it, didn't she?"

"Yes."

"Tell me about it."

He combed his hair in front of the mirror.

"She was going through a Pascin phase. She came to the bordello to sketch—and was enchanted by my beauty—she said. She paid like everyone else, but instead of screwing me, she painted me. She came several times. Madame forbid me to go to her studio to pose. She wouldn't profit from that. But I went anyway and after a while Maxi invited me to her home. I even became pals with her son. But then I did something stupid, I stole a gold bracelet and sold it. I also stole that painting. It was the only good thing that ever came out of my life…

"I didn't see Maxi again until a few days ago. She wanted the painting back. I told her it was long gone. She asked me to dinner. For old times sake, she said."

He pulled out a pack of cigarettes. "I'm going to smoke now. If you're sensitive you better leave."

I was, and at the moment, it was useless to try to get more out of him.

As he was shutting the door, he said casually, "Why don't you look into that old hotel on your street?"

Walking toward the Metro, I realized that was just what I had asked Boris to do.

I thought about what Arnaud had told us. Then it hit me that the five former child prostitutes he spoke about, all had some connection to the stolen paintings—and four of them were dead. Was Arnaud next on the list?

When we got back, Sol and Pascal were in Dimitri's back yard playing with a soft bat and a tennis ball, wearing Yankee baseball caps, stylishly back to front. I sat down to watch on an old wooden wine crate Dimitri had put out for Sol.

"You should see this kid hit. Hey, slugger, who won the triple crown for the old Cardinals?"

"Ducky Medwick," said Pascal.

"Incredible! Hey, why don't we all go to Mcdonald's for some fries?"

"Oui-yes, yes! Macdo's!"

Between me and Sol, this kid would learn English, and baseball. Sol actually looked happy. Maybe it brought back the days when he was the manager for our Sammy's little league team. But my anxiety for Boris was gnawing at my happy memories.

CHAPTER TWENTY EIGHT

That night the hurdy-gurdy woman serenaded us from the street. Her tuneful Breton song seasoned our romantic candle-lit dinner, but it was not without ominous undertones. It was a song I had heard so many times that I knew it by heart, but now I thought about the words.

A Paris la plus grande ville
Dans la plus belle maison
On dit qu'il ya-t-une barbiere
Cent fois plus belle que le jour

I couldn't help wondering if the beautiful "barbiere", female barber, had another occupation, as in the story of "Sweeny Todd." For a moment I felt goose bumps on my arms. But I rubbed them away. I didn't let my thoughts spoil our meal.

Sol and I made up. It had taken a little French kid, a lively tune from Brittany and a nice red Bordeaux that Maxi had given us to make our peace.

After the dishes were washed we relaxed in the glow from the wine. Sol's day had been good for a change.

"That Pascal's some kid," he told me, as if I didn't know.

"He's okay."

Sol scratched his head. "Funny thing."

"What?"

"It's nothing."

"What's nothing?"

"You know that old hotel next door to Dimitri's house? You know, the one where all those little North African kids live?"

The glow drained out of me. "What about it?"

"When I was teaching Pascal to play baseball in the yard, for just a split second I saw an old man with a beard through one of the windows—who reminded me of Boris."

"Boris is not an old man. And anyway, there are a lot of old men with beards around. Which window?"

"Upstairs somewhere. I can't remember. I don't have a camera in my head like you do. Sorry. I shouldn't have mentioned it."

"Talking about Boris, I learned something today that I have to pass on to him. I'll just take a minute to make the call."

"Please Goldie. Call tomorrow. We're having such a nice time together. We haven't had an evening to ourselves in a long time. Can't you forget about Boris just for tonight?"

I felt very uneasy, but I gave in for the sake of our relationship. "Okay Solly, I'll call him in the morning. Let's put on the tape of Glenn Gould playing the Goldberg Variations."

"A nice idea."

Next morning, Sol went out to buy the croissants and while he was out, I called Boris. I wanted to to tell him about the meeting with Arnaud, and I wanted to know what he'd found out about the ancient hotel. Maxi answered the phone.

"Boris isn't here. Another one of those all night affairs. It's getting tiresome."

I didn't like this piece of information one bit. In fact it gave me a punch in my kishkas.

"Do you know where he is, Maxi?"

"No, besides being married and sharing children we lead separate lives."

"I hope your life doesn't include Arnaud Duvier."

"I could do without your nagging. By the way, did you find him?"

"As a matter of fact I did. As a matter of fact I saw a painting of him you did in your Pascin period."

"That bastard! He told me he sold it years ago."

"Tell me about that painting," I said.

"I don't want to talk about it."

"Talk anyway," I told her.

I heard a big sigh. "After I put myself out for that bastard and let him play with my children, he stole that painting and a family heirloom. Are you satisfied?"

"Arnaud said you painted him in the brothel where he lived. Is that true?"

"Yes, it's true," she said.

"Tell me about the brothel."

"I was only there a couple of times, to paint Arnaud. The reception was a fin de siecle fleshmarket. Tiffany lamps, curlicued wrought iron, Rosetti paintings, the works. The prostitutes were lounging around in period costumes from all countries, waiting to be selected. The rooms of pleasure ranged from harems with odalisques to dungeons with torture racks and eunuchs. That woman had a sick imagination, but it paid off. Her customers were high officials in the government, members of the aristocracy—men and women. She must have made her fortune many times over."

My heart was racing. "Who was she, Maxi."

"She called herself Princess Polina Gregoryevna Romanov. To me she was a flamboyant, greedy old tart with bright red hair out of a bottle. She was insane, except when it came to making money. I don't want to talk about it any more. It's too sick."

"I have to know, Maxi!"

"Okay, okay, don't get hysterical. She told everyone she was the daughter of Alexandra, Tsarina of Russia—and that her father was

Rasputin. Can you imagine? And she wasn't joking! She actually believed that nonsense!"

"Did you ever tell this to Boris."

"God the questions you ask! I don't remember. Probably not. We didn't talk much in those days. Anyway, Madame Polina Gregoryevna and her evil Bordello are long gone. Can we stop this conversation? The thought of the way she abused those children makes me ill."

"And where was this brothel?"

"I'm surprised Arnaud didn't tell you. In that old hotel across the street from you."

"Oh, my God…Boris," I whispered. I had sent him to find out about that place—Daniel in the lion's den, with no thorn in its paw—and it was my fault.

"What did you say about Boris?"

"Nothing, nothing."

"Listen, Maxi, I have to go now. Take care of yourself."

"I always do."

When I put down the phone my hand was shaking. I had one thought—I had to get into that hotel. I had a terrible feeling that Boris was held prisoner there—and I kept seeing the faces and tattoos on the arms of the dead.

"Not Boris!" I cried out.

I couldn't panic. I had to think of a way of getting him out of there. I had to confront Polina Gregoryevna Romanov. Was she still alive, holed up somewhere in the old hotel or a nearby building? Who could she be? Someone I knew? I pulled the faces of women out of my file. The hurdy-gurdy woman? Why not? She was the right age. She lived near the old hotel. She had an aura of mystery around her. I grabbed wildly at things. Jeannine, the woman at Dimitri's castle had red hair. Not Boris' sister, she wouldn't hurt her own brother. Maybe the Madame was a man?

Then I felt myself grow cold as an image tumbled out of my files—an image of a little old lady in black handing out candy to little children—a woman I saw in the street every day. A woman I wanted to invite to tea.

I remembered the faces of the children in the back window of the hotel—the day I was trapped in the yard. Were they under the spell of Polina Gregoryevna Romanov, a lethal spider I knew as Madame Clara?

I was still in shock when I heard Sol coming up the stairs with a bounce in his step. He walked in holding Pascal's hand. Pascal kissed me and handed me a paper sack.

"I guess you were wondering why it took me so long to buy croissants."

"I wasn't wondering." I tried to look cheerful.

"I got lucky-Dimitri asked me to babysit again today.

After breakfast we're going to play baseball in the Tuilleries Gardens where there's more space for this slugger."

I was glad it was the Tuilleries and not the back yard of the old brothel. "Good idea. Just hide the equipment and look innocent when the cops walk by."

"We're just using a tennis ball."

"That's alright, then." I was wracking my mind for a way to get into the old hotel. Then I remembered that Dimitri's house shared the same yard. I would ask for his help again.

"Is Dimitri home now?" I asked Sol.

"No, he's gone. He told me he has something very important to do this morning. I told him to take his time."

"Damn," I whispered.

"Watch your language in front of the boy. Hey, don't worry about us. Pascal likes me, we'll be fine," he said as he put Dimitri's keys on the mantle.

It didn't take much to make Sol happy. Just a ball and bat and a little kid to teach.

Sol had bought milk and cocoa for Pascal's breakfast. I put my anxieties on hold while we ate.

When Sol left with Pascal, he forgot to take Dimitri's keys. He never remembers details like that. As I put them in my purse, the phone rang.

It was Maxi again.

"Something's happened to Boris."

"What?" I tried to keep the fear out of my voice.

"I don't know. I just got a phone call from him. He started to say something and then he made a funny noise and we were cut off."

"Maxi, did you call the police?"

"What could I tell them? Think about it. I have to find him myself."

"You're not going to see Arnaud, Maxi!"

She hung up.

I was sure now that Boris was in the old hotel. The thought terrified me. I left my terror in the apartment when I walked out. I had a date with Princess Polina Gregoryevna Romanov and I had to keep up my courage.

CHAPTER TWENTY NINE

Out in the street I got tangled up with the North African kids playing a kind of hide and seek. I untangled myself and looked up at Madame Clara's window to see if she was watching. She wasn't. I looked for a code on the door. There was none. Instead, there was a vertical line of doorbells with no names. Taking a deep breath I pressed the bell that coincided with her window. I got no answer. Maybe she wasn't there— or maybe she knew it was me. I tried to squelch my fear, determined to get inside whether she was there or not. I pressed each bell in turn. I heard no answering buzz. Of course, the adults were at work and the kids were out playing. And Madame Clara…?

I had the key to Dimitri's house in my purse. I hesitated. I wasn't so happy about breaking and entering as they say, but I had to. I reluctantly walked to his door, unlocked it and went in. Inside, my shoes clicked on the marble harlequin floor as I walked to the back and unlocked the door to the yard. Outside, the bases Sol had scrawled into the hard dirt were still there: home, first and third. There was no space for second. I approached the back of the hotel and looked at the ground floor window. No faces were pressed against the pane, but the window was still open a crack.

I pushed the wooden wine crate against the wall and climbed on it. The window groaned as I pushed it open the rest of the way. I paused to see if anyone had noticed. No one challenged me. After a moment, I climbed inside. This was not so easy for a person of my age in a tight skirt, but I made it.

So far so good, but I couldn't stop my jaw from trembling.

Inside, rumpled cots were crowded together, with dirty sheets and a few articles of children's clothing strewn about. Could this be the room that once held reclining odalisques? If so, nothing of them remained, except the faint outline of a figure on a wall, and the smell of unwashed children mingled with traces of memories. I stood there for a moment, then took a step forward. The floor creaked. I stopped. Silence. I continued on, squeezing between the cots, sickened by unwanted thoughts, until I reached the door.

The floor groaned. This time my feet panicked and went into spasm. They didn't want to walk out the door. They didn't want to be there at all. I removed the shoes from my rigid feet and stuffed them into my purse.

I ordered my bare feet to walk. They obeyed as my splayed toes slowly relaxed. I was in the hall now, painfully negotiating the gray wooden stairs, ignoring their musical accompaniment. If Madame Clara was in the house and heard me, she kept it a secret. I felt like I was walking forever, counting each step. But it was only two floors up where she kept watch at her window. There was only one door on that floor and it was open. I looked into a large, dark room, trying to control my fear.

Hanging on the far wall was a vision from one of my nightmares, a luminous blue crucifix—the model for the tattoo on the arms of the murder victims. I froze. Below the crucifix was an altar with candles burning on it. Kneeling in front of the altar was a garish figure praying out loud in in a strange language.

It was Princess Polina Gregoryevna Romanova just as Maxi had described her wearing a maroon velvet dress from another century. Her bright red hair flowed wildly about her head as she stood up and turned languidly toward me holding out her hand as though I was an honored guest.

She was tiny. Her dress was cut low over her scrawny bosom. Around her ashen neck she wore a necklace of rubies, like glistening drops of blood. Under spots of rouge, I saw a delicate face crumpled into fine lines.

As she floated toward me in slow motion, I saw her eyes, bright points of the palest cerulean blue. She came closer, and the details of her face came into focus. I had seen that face before, a younger version of it, on a portrait, in the attic of Dimitri's castle. I was overwhelmed by her flowery perfume. I tried to stop shivering.

Her delicate hand was of a twenty year old who had never done a day's work. I took it. The grip was remarkably strong as she drew me into the room. I tried to pull away, but she wouldn't let me go. A tall thin man in a uniform out of Anna Karenina entered, locked the door behind him with a key and slid an iron bar over it.

I didn't recognize him at first, but as I stared at at those hard eyes I was overcome with the sickening realization that he was Gregory—the caretaker at Dimitri's castle. I felt the floor rise as Madam Clara loosened her grip and threw my hand away like a used kleenex tissue.

Gregory looked at me with hatred, his black eyes slits in that old parchment face. He took my discarded arm with the grip of an iron vise and threw me into a chair, then he picked up a purple silk scarf and began clawing at it. I could feel that he was aching to strangle me. I kicked at him with my useless bare feet that were going into a cramp again.

"Non, laissez." she told him.

She sat down across from me in a blue velvet armchair and said in heavily accented English, "Talk to me, my darling. It is long time since I have conversation with intelligent person. You are intelligent person, no?"

"Brilliant," I whispered, my jaw almost in spasm.

"I frighten you?"

She wiped the rouge off her face with a lace handkerchief, put on a black cloak and covered her red hair with a black shawl.

She was the mousy Madame Clara again, the Madame Clara I wanted to invite into my home for tea. It was a good thing I didn't, she might have put poison in my cup.

"Don't be frightened, my darling, I won't let Gregory hurt you."

My eyes darted around the room, but my mind was enclosed in a bubble of fear. I focused on the stone mantlepiece with framed photos of a blond baby—a blond adolescent playing with a yellow dog in a field-and a grown man with a blond pony-tail.

Dimitri!

Then I saw a camera with a telescopic lens next to a copper samovar on a table. She had been photographing Dimitri. Why? Would he be victim number five? I stiffled a cry.

Then I heard a groan that seemed to be coming from behind a door at the far end of the room and I remembered why I was there.

I steadied my voice and asked, "Madame Clara, where is Boris?"

"We will speak of that peasant later. Talk to me. You were looking at the picture. A handsome boy, no?"

He couldn't have been one of her child prostitutes. The possibility was too painful, and I had seen no trace of a tattoo on his arm when he was working in his studio with his shirt off.

"Why do you have pictures of Dimitri?"

"I am a great admirer of beauty," she said.

"And the baby pictures?"

"You ask too many questions."

"You wanted me to talk to you," I reminded her.

"Yes. Talk, but not about pictures."

But I could not take my eyes off them. Dimitri was not in danger, I told myself. He could not have been one of her child prostitutes. They had all been damaged and diminished in some way. Not Dimitri, he was whole and perfect. I looked into Madame Clara's eyes, those pale blue eyes that were staring at me. I had seen them before-on Dimitri, Alexi, and Pascal. The truth slowly began to rise before my eyes.

Madame Clara was Dimitri's mother!

She didn't take her eyes off mine. She knew the truth had been revealed to me.

"You have courage," she said. "But Dimitri will never find out. You will never tell him, my darling."

I was in a dangerous spot, but as long as I could keep her talking about anything at all, I'd be safe from Gregory's iron claws.

"You are terrified that Dimitri might find out that you are his mother. You don't want him to know how you made your money. But I know-from the innocent bodies of little children."

Gregory came toward me.

"Pas encore!"

"You are wrong. They were my beautiful babies. I found them discarded like garbage in gutter. Out of garbage I created masterpieces for cream of society to enjoy. My beautiful babies had glorious life with me."

"Your son, Alexi, found out about your 'beautiful babies,' didn't he? That's why he ran away."

"Don't mention his name to me. He is no longer my son."

I looked at the mantlepiece. There were no pictures of the raven-haired Alexi, or her grandson Pascal on it.

"Who told Alexi about you? Was it Arnaud?" I asked.

"Arnaud? Arnaud did not have courage. No. It was Veronique!" She hissed the name. "I gave her everything. Because of me she became famous model, toast of art world. She spit on my kindness. She seduced Alexi and betrayed me. I do not wish to speak of Veronique!"

"Let's talk about Boris, then. What have you done with him?"

"The peasant is sleeping on my silk sheets. Sheets are more valuable than he is. I gave him lovely drug."

I almost panicked. "Not the poison Sylvie gave the clochard?"

"Poor Michel. No, not yet."

"Gregory," she said, "bring peasant who was looking for documents in Hotel de Ville."

"How did you know about that?" I asked

"I have friends everywhere. I am Romanov, and I am very rich. I can buy anything or anybody."

Gregory went into the back room. After a moment Boris staggered in, blinking. He didn't seem to notice me. Gregory pushed him into a chair.

Any hope I might have had that Boris could think of a way to get us out of there, faded. If only I could stall long enough, maybe Sol would remember he had seen Boris in the window. But I had convinced him it was his imagination. I looked at Boris. He seemed more awake now as he stared at Madame Clara with contempt. Maybe there was hope after all.

She stood up. "I am Polina Gregoryevna Romanov, daughter of Tsarina Alexandra."

"The Tsarina was no Romanov," he said, "she was German. She was Alix of Hesse. Unless your father was the Tsar, or a Romanov, you have no claim to the name."

Gregory snapped the silk scarf. She shook her head.

"Not yet."

I tried to divert their attention away from Boris.

"Was the Tsar your father?"

"No. My father was holy man, Rasputin!" She sat down.

So Maxi was right. Polina Gregoryevna really did believe that Rasputin nonsense.

Boris said, "Gregory Efimovich Rasputin was an illiterate peasant."

She seemed not to hear him. Her face suddenly became animated and her eyes turned black. She got up and walked the length of the room and back gesticulating as though performing on a stage. The woman was completely mad.

"The infidel nobles poisoned Rasputin, but he did not die—because of secret potion. They shot him and he did not die. The infidels tried to drown him in Neva River but he did not die. Now at last I have secret potion of eternal life. It took great effort of many people, but now I have it." Her face twisted into a grotesque smile.

Boris and I looked at each other.

"Where is this potion of eternal life, Princess?" Boris whispered.

"It is here, in escritoire, enclosed in Riza jewel." She pointed at a large, wide desk with doors."

We were suspended in a crystal of silence for a moment.

"Gregory, brandy! We drink toast to eternal life of Rasputin."

Gregory opened a small liquor cabinet and brought out an amber bottle.

"Not for me. I don't drink—not in the morning," I told her.

"You'll drink, darling. Time of day is nothing to you now. Don't worry I will not poison brandy. See? I take for myself."

Why were we just sitting there? Why didn't we get up and fight our way out? It was two against two. We didn't, I told myself, because the door was bolted, and Gregory had the key—and we were so close to the moment of revelation.

Gregory was moving toward me.

"Princess," I whispered, "did you grow up with the other children of the Tsarina?"

"No, and I didn't die with them in Ekaterinberg." She looked triumphant, held up her glass and downed the brandy. "I had my own suite in cellar of castle with my own servants. Papa came to visit every day. He was playmate, not saintly holy man who influenced course of history through Tsarina. To me he was beloved father who was taken away from me and thrown into River Neva.

"When Bolsheviks came, my mother's faithful servant, Gregory's father, brought me to France with our jewels. Castles were cheap. A crown bought a castle. Drink, my darling. It will soften pain."

Pain? What pain? What was she planning for us? I pretended I was taking a sip.

"Oh hell," said Boris and downed his, then held out the glass for more.

"Gregory fill glass."

I had come to this lunatic asylum to find Boris and I had found him. He was being held prisoner because he was snooping around the mairie. I didn't know what he discovered and I was in no position to ask. I was a prisoner because I knew too much, that was obvious. Silence, at the moment was dangerous, yet I needed space to think. There were things in my mental file I had to review. Boris would have to take over and keep the conversation going. He seemed to understand.

I laid out my files. Jacques, Michel the clochard, Veronique, Sylvie. Four of Madame Clara's five child prostitutes had been murdered. Five of Madame Clara's child prostitutes had connections with the stolen paintings. Madame Clara hired them. Madame Clara had them killed. It was all there in the files. Boris must have figured it out too.

Madame Clara was not stupid. She knew we knew. We were a threat to her alive. We were surely next in line for Gregory's scarf. Veronique and Sylvie had been strangled with a scarf—a scarf like the one Gregory was kvetching.

But we still didn't know everything. What was left? Madame Clara's motivation. For that we needed to know what paintings had been stolen. I shuffled through my files. Could they be the Rembrandt and Cezanne I had seen in the Castle attic? They were small enough to fit in the statue.

Then an image fell out of my files. It was of Arnaud telling me that a strange religion had been practiced in the bordello. Strange to him perhaps, but Madame Clara was obviously Russian Orthodox and believed, or pretended to believe that her father was the religious fanatic Rasputin. She had icons in her castle attic. She surely prayed in front of icons.

Icons were small enough to fit into the statue of Bathsheba!

I knew now what we were looking for, but what use was the knowledge unless we could find the icons and return them to the Russians. Only then would Boris escape their deadly wrath.

I was determined to get the truth out of Polina Gregoryevna Romanov if they were the last words I heard. But how? I looked at

Gregory who was so anxious to get his hands on me. The only way to find out was to ask.

"Tell us about the icons, Princess Polina Gregoryevna, the icons you wanted so badly you killed four people."

A look of disdain spread across her face as she answered me.

"I killed nobody. I am royalty. I show pleasure or displeasure. Others wish to please me. I don't want to know what they do, and and they don't tell me. I read what happens in newspaper, like everyone else."

"So you ordered the killings in your own way. Tell us about the icons you arranged to have stolen from the vaults of the Hermitage Museum."

"Stolen?" She looked genuinely surprised. "But Madame, they are mine—stolen by Bolsheviks. Icons were given to sainted father by mother. My darling mother kept them in Federov Cathedral in Tsarsko Selo. Did you know her favorite Saint was Seraphim of Sarov? I grow old now. Life fades. It was necessary I recover icons also for secret potion in jewels embedded in Riza icon."

That secret potion again! "May I see them?"

"But of course. I am proud to show. Gregory, open escritoire."

Gregory separated a key from the bunch attached to his belt by a chain and opened the door of the desk. We were looking at three incredible, glowing paintings. No wonder the Russians would do anything to get them back. For a moment I forgot our predicament.

"My treasures."

They were stunning. They represented the salvation of Boris. Or else the golden path leading to his grave, and mine. I kept the conversation going.

"The icons are fantastic. I'd love to hear all about them."

"Of course, my darling." She gestured. "This icon is Byzantine from eighth century. It survived destruction by iconoclasts. This is from Novgorod school. And this is my darling Riza, from seventeenth century."

The last was painted almost entirely in gold, except for the hands and face of the saint, and it was incrusted with precious jewels.

"Some of the jewels in Riza hold elixer to eternal life."

I suddenly felt a crazy spurt of hope. Maybe the Russian agent who was spying on me had seen me come in. Maybe he would realize that the paintings he was searching for were here, and call the police. But how could he have seen me? I came in through the yard. The spurt fizzled.

Boris was looking pretty alert now. He turned to Madame Clara.

"You are old, Polina Gregoryevna Romanov. After you have drunk the elixer, nobody can harm you. Why don't you give the paintings to the Hermitage so the whole world can appreciate the treasures of your father."

"It is true, they cannot kill me, but they can put me in prison, which is worse."

"They wouldn't do that to a frail old woman."

Her eyes sparked. "I will never give up icons—Never!"

Boris gave an almost imperceptible shrug.

She walked to her blue velvet armchair and sank into it like a watchful spider. As I looked at Gregory hovering above us near the fireplace, I entered the sticky web of her children.

"Who was Dimitri's father?"

Gregory was worrying that scarf again.

"Who? So many came and went. I kept a stable of the most beautiful women in Paris but they preferred me because my soul was on fire even though I was no longer young."

"You don't know who he was?"

"An aristocrat, of course, his name is not important."

"Surely, your sons did not live with you here?"

"I sent my boys to my castle. Madame knows castle, she was there."

"Yes."

"Gregory and Jeannine took care of them. When boys grew up, I retired and gave them house next door."

"And then Alexi found out you were his mother."

"Yes," she said bitterly. "I had such hopes for Alexi. At fifteen he could paint like Da Vinci. I gave Arnaud gallery to show Alexi's paintings, but he had bad taste with other paintings. I took gallery from him and sent him far away. Alexi signed with good gallery. Fine people bought his paintings.

"Then Veronique told him I was monster who ate children and he believed and ran away to monastery. I do not need him. To me he is dead. I still have my Dimitri. I see him every day through window."

"You turned Veronique, an innocent child, into a prostitute," I told her.

"Veronique did as she liked! She always had to have man. Arnaud, and Alexi, and others. When they were gone she took Jacques—the only one of my babies who was my friend. I trusted him. He betrayed me when he went to live with that slut. After that I could not bear to have him near me, I could not bear to look at him again." Her face was filled with hate.

"But you hired him to smuggle the paintings into France?"

"I did. It was convenient. But I would not let him bring them to me. Arnaud was never my friend, so could not deceive me. That's why I hired him to bring me paintings."

"But after he sold out to the Russian agents, it was Sylvie who brought them to you, wasn't it? It was Sylvie who got Michel to steal them from Jacques. It was Sylvie who gave him permission to kill Jacques, her hated husband."

She did not deny anything I said.

"But why did you have Sylvie killed?"

"I killed no one. She drinks too much and talks too much."

"Did Gregory kill her?

"Ask Gregory. Enough talk. I go for walk now."

Gregory unbolted and unlocked the door.

Suddenly the downstairs doorbell rang out, a long wailing rope of a sound that didn't stop. Gregory took a gun out of his pocket.

CHAPTER THIRTY

The sound of the bell was abruptly cut off and replaced by a thunderous hammering on the downstairs door. None of us moved.

Then we heard a strange husky voice coming from the street.

"Maman, Maman, ouvrez la porte! C'est moi, votre fils Dimitri, Maman!"

I looked at Madame Clara's face. I saw a wash of horror brighten her eyes. Then they became milky, as though an opaque shroud had been thrown over them. A shudder went through her fragile body and she crossed herself.

"Maman, Maman, c'est moi, Dimitri!" The voice was even louder.

Polina Gregoryevna Romanov walked slowly to the table, picked up a small bottle, poured a drop of liquid into a glass and drank it. I looked at Boris. At that moment we could have escaped, but neither of us could move. We were statues riveted to the floor as the shouting faded away.

Polina Gregoryevna picked up a lighted candle, held it out in front of her, walked to the window and deliberately set fire to the curtains. A blazing wall flared up between herself and Dimitri. As she bowed her head, a blue tip of flame burst out and caught her hair. Gregory dropped the gun and smothered her flaming hair with his hands, then lifted her up and walked out of the room into the hallway.

The fire spread quickly and the room was ablaze.

Boris grabbed the icons and shoved them into my arms. I was still in a state of shock. "Take them out of here. Move it, Goldie. If they're destroyed, I'm dead. I'm going to see if there are any children in the building."

I ran down the stairs with the paintings in my arms and through the front door. Then I stopped. Dimitri was standing in front of me on the cobblestones, ashen. Beside him were Maxi and Arnaud. I hurried over to them then turned and looked at the hotel. Flames were spilling out of the window, licking the plaster off the facade. I stood next to the others, hugging the paintings, mesmerized by the blazing building. Then I noticed Gregory with Madame Clara in his arms approaching the end of the block. Dimitri was following them with his eyes—not moving.

Boris rushed out the door just as the fire engine and police pulled into the street.

"Goldie will tell you about it," he said to Maxi as he grabbed the paintings from me and disappeared.

I looked down the block at a policeman trying to take Madame Clara from Gregory's arms. He wouldn't give her up. An ambulance turned into the street and as soon as the back door was open, Gregory, still holding Madame Clara, entered it.

I turned to Dimitri. He was watching the departing ambulance.

I took his arm. "Come up to my apartment." He didn't move. He didn't take his eyes off the space where the ambulance had been.

"Goldie," said Maxie, "what happened to your shoes?"

I looked down. My feet were bare.

"There they are. Sticking out of your pocketbook. If I was you I wouldn't go barefoot on this street."

Typical New Yorker that I was, I had held on to my pocketbook through everything. I obeyed Maxi and slipped on my shoes.

"Let's go, Arnaud," Maxi said, giving him a shove in the direction of my building, "before the police notice us."

I took Dimitri's arm and eased him down the street and up the stairs to my apartment.

My guests sat down on the sofa. I looked at Dimitri. His pale, translucent face was expressionless.

"Would you like some Armagnac, Dimitri?" He turned to me, but didn't answer. I saw in his face the same eyes I had been looking at in the face of Polina Gregoryevna. His were almost empty.

I squeezed his hand. It was an ice cube.

"I don't know about anyone else, but I'd like some Armagnac," Arnaud said.

"I would also," said Maxi. I looked at Dimitri. His eyes were completely empty now.

"Arnaud. Help me get him upstairs so he can lie down."

"No," Dimitri said.

I was afraid for him. "Maybe I should call a doctor?"

"I'll be alright." I didn't think so, but what could I do? My mind was too exhausted from the ordeal I had been through to argue with him.

"How did you know we were in there, Maxi?"

"I didn't. I guess I better explain. After I spoke to you about my fears for Boris, I went to see Arnaud. Dimitri and I got there at the same time—do you mind my telling Goldie about it, Dimitri?"

His voice was thin. "I don't mind."

"Dimitri came prepared to wring the truth out of him about his parents. But he didn't have to. Arnaud gave it to him with both barrels. He told him about his mother and her horrible sexual abuse of children, especially Veronique. He told him his mother had ordered the theft of three icons and had caused the deaths of four of her former child prostitutes, including Veronique.

"While Arnaud was talking, Dimitri was quiet. When he finished, Dimitri turned into a wild man. I thought he was going to kill Arnaud, but he didn't. He rushed out and grabbed a cab. We followed him in another. When he got here, he started yelling like a crazy man—like a little boy who needed his mother."

The downstairs doorbell buzzed, interrupting Maxi's story. It was Boris. He told us the paintings were safely in the hands of the Russians. There would be no international incident. He was off the hook. He was on his way to see Inspector Potiron.

"Well, that's finished then," I said.

"Not for me," said Dimitri.

CHAPTER THIRTY ONE

"You're shivering, Dimitri, you have to warm up," I told him. "I insist on making you a cup of tea."

"Yes."

I went into the kitchen and put the kettle on. Then I sat down on the couch and tried to unwind.

"You forgot about the Armagnac," said Arnaud.

"I'll bring it with the tea." I told him. "Listen Arnaud, something puzzles me. You knew from the beginning who had the paintings. Why didn't your Russian friends go after you instead of me and Boris?"

"They did. But they didn't get anything out of me. I knew I'd be dead if I told them about Polina Gregoryevna. The Russians couldn't lean on me too hard because of my connections with the French police, so they decided to work on you instead. They're not so dumb. They ended up getting what they wanted.

"I only went along with them as far as that business in the cellar. There was nothing in it for me anymore so I got the hell out of it."

The kettle was screaming to be taken off the stove. I stood up lazily and put verveine tea in a pot. Then I poured tea for Dimitri and myself and served Armagnac to the others.

As Dimitri drank his tea, the color slowly came back into his face.

"I need to see…my mother…before she dies."

"She's pretty tough. She probably won't die until she chooses to," I told him.

"I think she already made that decision."

"Then I'll go with you," I said.

Dimitri got up. He was pretty unsteady.

"Just let me leave a note for Sol."

As we walked toward the hospital, Dimitri murmured, "Madame Clara...my mother is Madame Clara. That was why she was always following me with her eyes."

"She calls herself Polina Gregoryevna Romanov."

"I will never really know who she is."

"Her story's so wild it's hard to know what part of it is true."

"I only know that she's evil, an evil old woman. I know now why Alexi ran away."

A policeman was guarding the hospital room. Princess Polina Gregoryevna Romanov was lying in bed looking tiny and vulnerable in a white gown. White bandages covered her burnt hair. The room smelled of ointment and burn and flowery perfume. The curtains were drawn and in the dim light her pupils covered most of the blue of her irises. Her eyelids were unblinking. Gregory, who was sitting beside her, got up and left without looking at us.

Dimitri took Gregory's place. I stood at the door while he looked closely at her face, as though he could solve the mystery hidden there. He had known her, spoken to her in passing, seen her grow old without noticing. She had been part of the scenery of his adult life without his knowing she was his mother. Had there ever been a tug at his heart that linked him to her? Two people of the same clay? He formed the word "maman" with his lips, but did the word have resonance for him?

He picked up her small hand, measured it with his own, then put it down.

"Maman," he said softly.

Her body shuddered.

"Maman," he said. She drifted further away. He seemed to want to tell her something before she died. He made an effort to speak. His French was simple enough for me to understand. He told her that God loved what was left of the little child in her that was still pure. He said that God would forgive her, even if he couldn't. She didn't react. Her breathing became raspy.

He stood up and went into the hall. He stopped a nurse and told her to find the priest, his mother was dying.

"She is not dying, only very tired," the nurse said.

"She is my mother, and she is dying, she must see a priest, he must give her absolution. Hurry."

Was it possible there was a faint thread of connection between them?

When the priest arrived Gregory was with him. He prepared to do the things priests do. I didn't want to watch, so I found a lounge and looked out over the roofs of Paris. Dimitri had known his mother for just a few moments and for the rest of his life he would keep this bitter memory of her.

After a while Dimitri came and told me it was all over. His eyes were dry. We walked out into the late summer afternoon, and home. The air of rue Abbe Etienne was suffused with the smell of the fire.

When Sol arrived with Pascal we had composed ourselves enough to function. Pascal was flushed and messy from playing ball. He jumped into Dimitri's lap and gave him a good American hug, not the usual peck on each cheek. Dimitri hugged back for a long time. Then he put Pascal down and went upstairs to the bathroom.

Sol, sensing something was up, took out his chess set and went into the back room with Pascal.

Dimitri stayed upstairs for quite a while, and when he came down he told me, "I've decided to sell the castle and the houses in Paris."

"But where will you go?"

"To the sea. Perhaps Treguier in Brittany, or maybe Honfleur in Normandy. But first I must see Alexi and tell him everything. He will listen, though he will not talk to me."

"Maybe after you've had a chance to distance yourself, you'll feel differently about such a drastic change."

"I don't think so."

"What will you tell Pascal?"

"Bit by bit he will know everything. I'll start by telling him about his father. We'll visit Alexi when we can. Alexi won't be able to resist the boy. And one day they'll understand each other.

"You decided all that just now?"

"Yes. We'll go now. Thank you for your kindness."

"Listen, stay for dinner. Stay overnight. It must smell terrible in your house from the fire.

"We have to be by ourselves."

Dimitri interrupted the chess game. The two of them said goodby and left, hand in hand.

"Goldie. What the hell is going on?"

I told him everything and was left with another case of shock on my hands. But Sol was over it by the time Boris arrived, exhausted.

Boris had finished with Inspector Potiron. He assured me I wouldn't be bothered anymore. He told us Gregory was in the police station spilling out his guts. He didn't care about his own life now that his princess was dead. He had been loyal. He had murdered those who were a threat to her.

"Not Sylvie," I said. "He was at the castle when Sylvie was murdered. I know, I was there."

"It's a six or seven hour drive to Paris the way they drive in France. He could easily have done it, especially at night when there isn't much traffic."

"Now you mention it, Jeannine drove us to the station that morning. And Veronique?"

"On one of his frequent visits to his princess."

Thinking about Veronique, I was overcome with sadness.

"Gregory suddenly changed," Boris told us. "He became a madman, raving that the Princess was not really dead because she had drunk the elixer of immortality. The Inspector didn't know whether to send him to prison or to the loony bin. Let's take a walk, Goldie."

"Sure."

Sol didn't seem to mind when Boris and I walked out together hand in hand—or maybe he was still stunned by my revelations.

We ended up near the ancient carousel above Les Halles.

"This used to be the big Parisian produce market that served onion soup to the likes of Hemingway and Fitzgerald," Boris told me as we arrived.

"I know. I missed out on it. The first time Sol and I came to Paris it was a giant hole in the ground."

"Maxi and I used to come here and have onion soup. That was when we were courting, but we never saw anyone famous."

I laughed at the word, 'courting.'

"I'll never really know Maxi if I live to be Methuselah's age," Boris said.

"Sol's an open book."

"Are you sure, Goldie?"

"Now you mention it, I'm not."

"Let's go for a ride on the carousel and pretend we are six years old," he said.

"Pretend? I am six years old."

We paid our ten francs each and got on the two most beautiful horses on the merry-go-round, side by side, and tried to forget, for a moment, the evil daughter of Rasputin, who had momentarily shattered our worlds.